WALK
TILL YOU
DISAPPEAR

WALK
TILL YOU
DISAPPEAR

JACQUELINE DEMBAR GREENE

KAR-BEN
PUBLISHING

KAR-BEN PUBLISHING™
An Imprint of Lerner Publishing Group, Inc.
241 First Avenue North
Minneapolis, MN 55401 USA
Website address: www.karben.com

Jacket illustrations by Odessa Sawyer.

Main body text set in Bembo Std Regular.
Typeface provided by Monotype Typography.

Library of Congress Cataloging-in-Publication Data

Names: Greene, Jacqueline Dembar, author.
Title: Walk till you disappear / Jacqueline Dembar Greene.
Description: Minneapolis : Kar-Ben Publishing, [2019] | Series: Kar-ben books
    for older readers | Summary: Twelve-year-old Miguel, who feels drawn to the
    priesthood, is shocked to learn of his Jewish ancestry and runs away into the desert
    where he meets Rushing Cloud, a Tohono O'odham youth escaping a mission
    school. Includes historical notes and glossary. | Includes bibliographical references.
Identifiers: LCCN 2018045013 (print) | LCCN 2018051276
    (ebook) | ISBN 9781541561274 (eb pdf) | ISBN 9781541557222 (th : alk. paper) |
    ISBN 9781541557239 (pb : alk. paper)
Subjects: | CYAC: Coming of age—Fiction. | Prejudices—Fiction. | Runaways—
    Fiction. | Ranch life—Arizona—Fiction. | Jews—United States—Fiction. |
    Tohono O'odham Indians—Fiction. | Indians of North America—Arizona—
    Fiction. | Arizona—History—To 1912—Fiction.
Classification: LCC PZ7.G834 (ebook) | LCC PZ7.G834 Wal 2019 (print) | DDC
    [Fic]—dc23

LC record available at https://lccn.loc.gov/2018045013

Manufactured in the United States of America
1-46139-45744-12/17/2018

CONTENTS

To the Sephardim and the Native
Americans who walked a shared path

CHAPTER 1
Making Plans

"That's a stupid story, Berto. You're just trying to scare us," Miguel said, buffing the silver incense burner until it gleamed.

Alberto put two fingers up against his head as if he had sprouted horns. He loomed over Miguel and scowled. "Beware of Israelites with devil's horns," he intoned in a deep voice. Miguel squirmed as his friend's lanky body towered over him.

"You made that up," Miguel insisted.

"It's true, I swear," Berto protested. "My father told me he's seen them."

"I don't believe you, either," Luis said with a nervous laugh. He looked toward the altar at the front of the church. "Let's ask Father Ignacio. He'll know." The three friends approached quietly as the priest swept sand from the floor around the low altar.

Miguel set the polished incense burner on a small table. "*Padre*," he asked hesitantly, "is it true that Israelites have devil's horns?"

The priest stopped in mid-sweep. "Where did you hear such a foolish tale?" he asked, his eyes widening a bit. He leaned against the handle of the straw broom and gazed at the boys from under his heavy eyelids. His face was long and thin, and creases ran from the sides of his nose down toward his drooping mouth. "While nonbelievers will be denied entrance to Heaven, they are not devils on Earth."

Miguel punched his companion's arm lightly. "I told you!" he exclaimed.

Berto shook his head. He lowered his voice and said ominously, "My father told me that he has seen them with his own eyes, *Padre*."

"If your father saw such a thing, Alberto, it must have been in a dream. In any case, you have nothing to fear, for Jesus will protect you. Now, if you've finished your work for today, go on home—and no more tales." The boys shuffled between the pews toward the church's open door.

Stepping into the sunlight, Miguel gazed back into the cool shadows. Wooden statues of saints lined the walls like silent sentinels. Miguel knew each familiar carved and painted figure, and felt each had its own personality. The saints always seemed to listen to every murmured prayer, standing in the haze of incense that burned inside the adobe mission.

Father Ignacio followed the boys outside. A small knot of Papago women walked along the plank sidewalk on Tucson's main street. They bent forward against the weight of the rope baskets that hung from a band across their foreheads and rested against their backs. The woven burden baskets were filled with earthen *ollas* to sell. The women's barefoot children followed behind, each carrying one or two of the empty water jugs. They would have many eager customers, since all the settlers in the territory depended on the clay jugs to keep water cool and fresh each day.

The women wore ragged, mismatched clothes, and the children were half naked, their skin coated with a thick layer of red desert dust. Miguel thought it seemed as if they, too, were made of clay. He pulled the brim of his straw hat lower over his eyes, trying to protect himself from the dust kicked up as they shuffled along the dry dirt road.

"*Hola, señoras,*" called the priest. "When the church bells announce Mass this Sunday, please come and worship with us." He forced a smile, but Miguel couldn't help noticing that even when Father Ignacio smiled, his long face looked sad. The Papago women trudged past without a word, and the children stared at the boys with their round, dark eyes.

"Do you think they will come, *Padre*?" asked Luis.

The priest rubbed his thumb absently over the thick wooden cross that hung against his brown, cowled frock. His gray-streaked beard seemed to quiver. "It's difficult persuading the natives to come to church. I must admit there are times when I begin to despair."

"But you've already converted lots of them," Miguel noted.

"Many of the peaceful Papago tribe have been baptized," the priest agreed, "but they keep their heathen practices even while proclaiming their Christian faith." Then he brightened. "But you are right, my son. At least they listen, and we will try to build a stronger devotion until they give up their superstitious ways."

Miguel had heard Father Ignacio preach that non-believers were destined to spend eternity in the fires of hell. Prickles raced along the back of his neck. Still, he was certain that more and more of the native people would accept the church's teachings. Those who did would be saved. *In this earthly life, they are heathens*, the priest often repeated, *but they have a chance to go to heaven in the next life.*

"I hope that someday I will become a priest," Miguel blurted out. "I can teach non-believers the truth." Berto and Luis exchanged a look of surprise, but Miguel knew they wouldn't dare tease him in front of Father Ignacio. It was time that his friends knew what Miguel hoped for.

Still, he couldn't escape remembering his father's discouraging words. *You don't belong in the church*, Miguelito, his father argued. *When you're older, you will understand.*

Miguel already understood what his father wanted from him. Papá only wanted Miguel to help run their horse ranch. As much as he loved the excitement of raising horses, the work was never-ending. Somehow, the quiet calm of the church drew him in. He imagined the satisfaction of saving souls. Why couldn't his father see that was more important than training horses?

Miguel snapped back from his concerns when he heard the priest's voice. "Becoming a priest isn't an easy decision. You must be patient," Father

Ignacio advised. "If God calls, you will know it in your heart."

Miguel watched the Papagos disappear around a bend in the road, their clay *ollas* clinking as they shifted in the burden bag. "I'll light a candle on Sunday and pray for their salvation," he offered.

Father Ignacio put his hand on Miguel's shoulder. "My little *padre*," he murmured. "Perhaps you do have a calling." Miguel fought a fleeting surge of pride. Still, Papá was not proud of Miguel's plans. It seemed he was always disappointing his father.

The priest smiled and stretched his arms wide, as if enveloping the three boys. "I am blessed to have such reliable altar boys. Be sure to come early on Sunday. There will be plenty to do before Mass."

"I—I don't know how early I can get here," Miguel stammered. "My brothers, or a ranch hand . . . that is, I have to wait for someone to ride with me."

"Why don't you bunk with me this weekend?" Luis offered. "Then you'll already be in town and we'll get to church early."

"But today is Friday," Miguel explained. "You know Mamá makes a big dinner on Friday nights. I have to be there." He shrugged. "You can't imagine how Mamá fusses if one of us is even a minute late!"

Father Ignacio looked intently at Miguel. "So, Fridays are the big meal of the week," he said evenly.

"With silver candlesticks, a lace tablecloth, and our best dishes," Miguel added. "Mamá and our housekeeper Carmella cook and bake on Friday mornings as if it was a holiday. By Saturday, my mother is so tired that she just rests on the porch, and we eat whatever is left over for dinner."

Miguel untied his chestnut mare from the hitching post and rubbed her nose gently. "*Vámanos, Alma,*" he said, leading the horse by the reins. "*Adiós, Padre.*"

The boys walked briskly along the rutted road. "You're so lucky to be able to ride every day," Luis said. His brown eyes sparkled beneath his floppy hat brim. "I wish I lived on a ranch, instead of over a store. The only time I get to ride is when my father sends me across town on the mule to deliver a sack of chicken feed." He scuffed his boot against the ground, kicking up a small mound of sand.

"But my father never lets me ride alone," Miguel complained. "He keeps telling me that when I turn thirteen I will be a man, but I'm almost thirteen and he still treats me like a baby. I'm already too old to have someone riding shotgun every time I leave the ranch."

"I guess your father's worried about Apaches," Luis said. "That's why my family opened their store inside Tucson's walls."

"Being in town is much safer," Berto said emphatically, but Miguel thought the horse ranch was safe enough. Apaches were only interested in stealing stallions, and they certainly wouldn't want Alma. The mare barely plodded along.

"I'm not afraid of Apaches," he boasted. "I could outride them anytime."

The boys continued along Main Street, skirting the low adobe buildings that all needed a fresh coat of paint. Soon Berto turned in at his family's café, its faded gingham curtains shading the lower portion of each window. The door to the café was open, and heat radiated from the wood cooking stove inside. A hand-lettered sign on the door read, "No Indians Allowed!" Miguel wondered if Berto's father would keep out Israelites too.

"*Adiós, amigo*," Miguel called, lapsing back into the comfort of Spanish.

Luis loosened the top buttons on his shirt. "I hope it's not this hot on Sunday," he said as they continued on. "It's stifling for April!"

The boys kept to the side of the road as wagons

loaded with supplies rattled past. Women in long skirts and wide-brimmed bonnets bustled in and out of the few shops along Main Street, carrying their purchases in straw baskets. Before long, Luis climbed the outside stairway that led to his family's rooms over their feed store.

He waved down to Miguel. "*Hasta Domingo*! See you Sunday!"

Miguel swung his leg up over the saddle and settled on his mare. He pushed his knees against her flanks, but Alma wouldn't be hurried. She plodded past the Park Brewery saloon, seemingly deaf to the raucous laughter and tinkling piano music from within.

"Eh, Miguel, what you think?" called a gravelly voice. Miguel pulled Alma to a halt. "Whoa, girl," he said.

Charlie Meyer stood on the edge of the street scrutinizing his shop window. Doc Meyer had moved to Arizona Territory from Germany and was the town's pharmacist as well as its justice of the peace. Although he wasn't really a doctor, everyone in Tucson willingly gave him the title for his ability to mix a potion to ease almost any ailment.

Miguel stared at the apothecary shop. Two large glass globes filled the window and reflected the bright sunlight. One ball was rosy red and the other a deep sky blue. The mysterious globes captivated Miguel. "They're beautiful, Doc. What are they?"

"Blown glass," the pharmacist said proudly. "They came all the way from Cally-for-nya in a wagon train without so much as a little crack!" He hooked his thumbs into his vest pockets. "It's a new idea to bring in the business. Once word gets around, people will come to my shop just to see them."

"But you're the only apothecary in Tucson," Miguel chuckled. "Where else could people go if they get sick?"

The pharmacist shrugged and stepped up onto the sidewalk so he was face-to-face with Miguel as he sat astride his horse. "Your Papá invites me tonight for dinner. Don Miguel says Friday night is your Mamá's best cooking of all the week." He flashed a mischievous grin beneath his bushy moustache. "Maybe a little poker we'll play afterwards, eh?"

"*Excelente!*" Miguel said, falling back into Spanish. It would always be his first language and came out whenever he got excited. "*Hasta la vista*—see you later!"

Miguel wondered how Fridays came to be the festive meal of the week at his home, instead of

Sundays. Father Ignacio had seemed a bit surprised, and his friends never understood why he had to be home for that meal above all others. Doc Meyer seemed amused by the invitation. Miguel always looked forward to it and had never questioned the tradition. *I guess every family has its own way of doing things,* he mused.

He clicked his tongue, and Alma ambled through the city gates toward the water well. He wondered who would be waiting there to meet him today. Miguel eased the mare around the women who had filled their *ollas* with fresh water and now balanced the heavy jugs on their heads. Their colorful skirts swayed against their bare ankles, and bright cotton *rebozos* shielded their faces from the strong sun.

As Miguel looked across the sea of festive colors, he saw his brothers. Esteban and Ruben stood together while their horses lapped water from a wooden trough. Miguel brushed the hair from his eyes with annoyance. Why didn't Papá trust him to ride home by himself? He especially hated having his brothers come to meet him. *Just because they're older and pack rifles on their saddles, they treat me like a little kid.* At least when Papá sent ranch hands, they talked and joked along the way as if Miguel were one of them.

He leaned close to Alma's head. "Let's sneak away," he whispered. "If they don't see us, perhaps we can ride home alone." The mare twitched her ears. Miguel turned the horse, but it was too late.

"*Ho, Miguelito!*" Esteban called, mounting his sleek stallion with a flourish. A black sombrero shaded his face and highlighted his trim moustache. He wore an embroidered shirt with narrow sleeves that reached to his black leather riding gloves. The young women at the well stole glances at him from behind their soft *rebozos*. Miguel could see his brother relish their admiring looks. "*Adiós, señoritas,*" Esteban called with a grin, and dark eyelashes fluttered at him.

Miguel's brother, Ruben, wasn't interested in impressing the Tucson women. At seventeen, he was two years younger than Esteban and wore work clothes even when he was away from the ranch. Ruben mounted his horse impatiently. "We've been waiting too long for you," he chided Miguel. "Where've you been?" Before Miguel could answer, Ruben galloped off. "*Vámanos, hermanos,*" he called.

Miguel and Esteban spurred their horses to catch up, and soon the three brothers rode along together, keeping an even pace.

"You don't have to ride into town for me," Miguel protested. "I can take care of myself—even without a rifle."

Esteban waved his arm toward the vast expanse of desert. Tall saguaro cactus dotted the landscape beside low *paloverde* trees with their lime-green bark. "Apaches can be hiding behind any rock or cactus you see, or a band of them can ride up out of nowhere. They'd kill us in a minute, just for the horses."

Miguel felt proud of his family's ranch. Every settler in the territory agreed there were few mounts that could match the spirit and speed of an Abrano horse. Each one was a cherished possession. Unfortunately, the Apaches agreed. The ranch hands constantly guarded against their raids, yet roving bands stole a number of valuable horses each year. Miguel knew that Papá was often counting his losses.

Ruben rode smoothly with his horse's gait while he talked. "They'd kill Esteban and me, but you're young enough to become part of the tribe," he told Miguel. "They'd keep you around."

Esteban laughed. "I can just see you in a pair of moccasins sneaking into the corral and stealing Papá's horses!"

"I'm faster than any Apache," Miguel boasted. "I could get away, especially if I was riding a stallion."

"You're dreaming, *Miguelito*," Esteban said, again calling him by the childish nickname.

"I'm not Little Miguel," he declared. "Stop treating me like a baby!" He kicked his heels into the mare's flanks, and she loped ahead. Miguel's hat flapped against his back, and his hair blew in the hot breeze. With his brothers behind him, Miguel could at least pretend he was on his own.

CHAPTER 2
An Unwelcome Visitor

Miguel looked ahead as he approached the ranch. Horses stood in the flat-fenced corrals that were built close to the spacious barn. Two cactus-wood ramadas made a shady covering to keep the hay and water troughs cool.

One of the ranch hands stood in the center of one corral, leading a young stallion through its paces. The pepper-gray yearling had a gentle disposition, and Miguel had been visiting it in the stalls, offering a piece of fruit or a sugar cube from his hand. It had come to recognize Miguel and let him rub its nose as he spoke to it quietly. How he would love to call that horse his own.

Farther out, a stand of tall cottonwood trees clustered near a watering hole, their green leaves stirring in the breeze. The desert scrub that stretched to the horizon was all part of the family's land.

As the brothers tied their horses to a corral rail, Miguel saw an unfamiliar wagon in the shade of the barn. It was loaded with bundles lashed together with a web of ropes.

"Why didn't you tell me we had visitors?" Miguel asked, but his brothers ignored him, removing their horses' saddles. Ruben began pumping water into a trough.

Miguel's thoughts rambled. *Maybe it's a family from a big city—like Chicago, or even Philadelphia,* Miguel thought. There were so many possibilities. *Maybe they have a boy my age!*

With no hotels in Tucson, and few ranches in the area, the Abranos often welcomed travelers to their home. Miguel loved meeting people from faraway places and hearing about the towns they had left behind. He would close his eyes and imagine what it might be like living someplace completely different than a ranch in the Arizona desert.

If I become a priest, he realized, *the church will surely send me to live in a new place.* It was an exciting thought, although his family wouldn't agree.

Esteban and Ruben started to rub down their

stallions, but Miguel couldn't wait to meet the travelers. He raced to the house, his boots clattering on the wooden veranda.

"Hey!" Esteban shouted. "Don't leave Alma like this."

Miguel was tired of following his brothers' orders. "I'll take care of her soon enough," he called. "She can wait."

He hurried off, pushing aside a nagging sense of guilt. Papá always said caring for your horse came before anything else. He believed that since the horses worked hard for us, we owed them nothing less than the best treatment.

"Don't think we're going to take care of her for you," Esteban retorted. Miguel ignored his brothers and let the smell of frying *bimuelos* lead him into the kitchen. Mamá and Carmella were dropping batter into sizzling skillets. Long white aprons protected their dresses, but they stood back from the spattering oil. Carmella's hair hung down her back in a thick black braid. Mamá's wavy hair was streaked with gray and was pinned up tightly at the back of her head. A damp ringlet fell across her forehead.

"Ah, *Miguelito*," Mamá greeted him. "I miss you when you are in school all day."

"I like being in town," Miguel said, snitching a cooling pastry coated in cinnamon and sugar. "Why, just today, Doc Meyer set up a window display with two big colored glass balls."

He held his arms in a huge arc to show his mother how large they were. "The whole street looks like a fiesta."

"*No me digas*—you don't say?" Mamá marveled. "Let's ask Doc Meyer to tell us about them when he comes for dinner tonight."

Miguel polished off the crispy *bimuelo* and planted a sugary kiss on his mother's cheek. He poured a glass of cool water from an earthen *olla*. "Who's visiting?" he asked.

Before Mamá could answer, Papá came into the kitchen with a travel-worn man. Miguel couldn't help staring at the stranger's bristly gray-flecked sideburns and the sparse beard that sprouted from his chin like sagebrush. While Papá wore a pale gray pinstriped suit, the visitor was dressed in black, with a round hat, a long coat jacket, and threadbare pants. A slim black ribbon of wrinkled silk served as a tie against his dusty white shirt. The man's clothes were far too heavy for the hot weather.

"Señor Jacob Franck, please meet my wife, Doña

Elena," Papá said. "And this is my youngest son, Miguel, and our housekeeper, Carmella."

The man looked solemnly at Mamá and bobbed his head. "It is most pleasing to meet you, Señora," he said in a raspy voice with an accent much like Doc Meyer's. He nodded at Carmella, and then turned in Miguel's direction and held out his hand. "Young man," he said. Miguel shook the man's hand reluctantly.

Mamá wiped her hands on her apron. "Why are you bringing guests into the kitchen?" she scolded Papá. "I was just about to send a tray of pastries and some fresh lemonade into the parlor."

"We're heading outside to sit under the ramada," Papá said. "It's cooler in the shade."

"Do you have your family with you?" Miguel asked, looking toward the parlor door.

"Señor Franck is traveling the territory alone, selling housewares," Papá explained. He turned to the stranger. "I'm sure it's a lonely life."

Mamá shook her head sympathetically. "We are pleased to welcome you to our home," she said.

"Señor Franck will be with us for several days," Papá said. "By the time he moves on, there won't be many ranches around without a new iron skillet or at least a packet of sewing needles." Miguel could barely hide his disappointment. He had expected a family of new settlers and had hoped to make a new friend.

Carmella filled two glasses with pale lemonade, set them on a tray with the platter of pastries, and carried it outside.

"Our friend Charlie Meyer is joining us for dinner tonight," Papá remarked to the guest. "He is a compatriot of yours, all the way from Germany."

A shadow of worry crossed the peddler's face. "I hope he won't mind sharing the table with a poor Jew." Miguel stiffened. Señor Franck was an Israelite!

"Don't worry," Papá reassured him. "In Arizona Territory all are welcome."

"Not every rancher is so kind," the peddler said. "Sometimes people are afraid if a stranger looks or sounds a little different. And me, I am different both ways!"

"As long as you're not an Indian," Papá joked, "you will be accepted."

"Jews and Indians," Señor Franck mused. "We have many things in common, especially since we are not like the settlers. Maybe the natives understand this and so they don't bother me when I travel." He gave a faint smile, revealing a row of crooked teeth. "Although it might just be the shiny buttons in my wagon. If I give them a few polished buttons, they are as happy as children with the peppermints!"

Papá chuckled, but Miguel heard nothing amusing in the man's words. He was different for more than his strange clothes and hair, and his grating voice. He was an Israelite, and yet Papá had invited the man to share their home. Miguel's heart raced. He was more afraid of having Señor Franck sleeping under his roof than he was of traveling across the desert alone.

Berto insisted that Israelites were devils in human form with horns sprouting from their heads. Father Ignacio said that was nothing more than a made-up story. Then why was the peddler wearing his hat indoors? Miguel stole a fearful glance at the top of the man's head, but he could see nothing poking out of the man's black hat except wiry hair springing in all directions.

Father Ignacio fretted over the Papago who came to Mass, yet still prayed to their own gods. At least they tried to follow the faith. The peddler was far worse. He didn't believe in the church teachings at all.

Maybe I can bring Señor Franck to Mass on Sunday,

Miguel thought. *If I can show him how wrongheaded his beliefs are, it might prove I have a calling.* He followed his father and the peddler outside and stood while they sat on carved wooden chairs under the ramada. Señor Franck took a sip of lemonade and reached for a *bimuelo* with gnarled fingers. He smiled with pleasure at the first taste.

"Nothing better than Mamá's cooking, eh?" he said to Miguel. "Even if you are growing faster than the agave stalk that shoots up before our eyes, you're still your Mamá's boy."

Miguel tensed under the peddler's steady gaze. Everything about Jacob Franck made him uneasy, from the sound of his voice to his odd appearance.

Miguel straightened his shoulders as if to defend himself against the man's words. "I'm turning thirteen next week," he said.

Jacob Franck nodded enthusiastically. "In my religion, this is the age of manhood." His eyes had a faraway look. "Back in my little village before my thirteenth year, I studied hard to become a bar mitzvah." Miguel was puzzled. What was the peddler talking about?

"This you don't know, eh?" the man commented. "When a Jewish boy turns thirteen, he is called up to read from our sacred Torah, reading the Hebrew words just the way they were first written down in the Old Testament. This is a big moment in life, for then he is a boy no longer. He is considered a man. It is to celebrate!"

Miguel didn't know what a Torah was, but he didn't much care. The peddler kept explaining. "Just as your church prays in Latin," he said, "we pray in Hebrew, the language of the Bible. It takes a lot of study."

Maybe Jews wrote their beliefs in Hebrew so no outsiders could understand their heathen words. Miguel looked steadily at Señor Franck. "If you'd like to come to Mass with us this Sunday, I can teach you some of the Latin prayers."

"Miguel!" Papá scolded. "We must always respect a man's beliefs, even when they are different from our own."

Miguel hung his head at Papá's rebuke. He never could seem to please his father. Couldn't Papá see that Miguel was trying to lead Jacob Franck to the church's teachings? Father Ignacio had dedicated his life to doing exactly that with all the non-believers, and Papá would never criticize the priest. So what had Miguel done to be scolded like that?

The peddler waved his hand nervously. "Nothing to worry, Don Mateo," he said. "Young Miguel is just a boy and still he is learning about the world."

Papá shook his head, and Miguel saw his father's disappointment. No matter how hard Miguel tried to please his father, Papá always found fault with him.

Jacob Franck looked out at the vast expanse of the Abrano ranch. "How did your family come to settle here?" he asked.

Perhaps this was Miguel's opportunity to make amends. He knew the family history perfectly from all the times that Papá had told about it since Miguel was a small boy. "Our family has bred horses on this land for more than three hundred years," he said.

Señor Franck raised his thick eyebrows with interest. "A rich heritage," he marveled.

"One of our ancestors came with the Spanish conquistadors," Miguel said proudly.

Papá leaned back in his chair. "Eventually, he became a mapmaker, charting the land for the first time. King Charles gave the Abranos this land in 1540 in gratitude for that service." He turned to Miguel. "So, *mijo*, did you water Alma and cool her down?"

"I'll make sure she's had plenty to eat," Miguel said, avoiding a lie. He took one more *bimuelo* from the plate and headed to the corral. His father's voice carried through the still air, complaining to the peddler. "When I was his age, I knew how to manage everything at the ranch. He knows horses, but he doesn't work hard enough."

Alma stood in the heat, her saddle still cinched tightly. Miguel hurriedly removed the saddle and shook out the blanket, setting them both on the corral railing. He pumped the trough full of fresh water and fed the mare his last bit of pastry. Miguel hoped his brothers didn't tell Papá that he had left the mare untended in the heat. He didn't need any more trouble today.

Alma nickered and pawed the ground as if she were complaining too. "Sorry, girl," he apologized. She was shedding her thick winter coat, and Miguel brushed her vigorously. He was always amazed at how the horses' coats changed color from winter to summer. Alma's soft dark hair was turning back to a glistening chestnut.

"Why would Papá invite Jacob Franck to stay at our ranch?" he asked the horse. "That man could be dangerous." He led Alma to her stall, removed her bridle, and filled a bucket with oats. "As soon as that peddler goes to the other ranches to sell his buttons and cloth, the entire town will know he's staying at our place." Miguel didn't know if he was more worried about having an Israelite under his roof or about what Berto and Luis would say when they found out.

As the mare ate, Miguel's thoughts turned to more practical matters. Since Papá saw that Señor Franck could travel the desert without being attacked by Apache raiders, maybe Miguel could use that to his advantage. If Papá was in a good mood at dinner, perhaps Miguel could persuade his father to let him ride to Tucson alone on Sunday morning. Maybe he'd let him take the pepper gray. Tonight might be the perfect time to ask. He would take a chance—tonight.

CHAPTER 3
Questions

Doc Meyer was delighted to meet a newcomer from the "Old Country," as he called it. The two men gripped each other's hands and began babbling in German. Miguel frowned at the harsh-sounding, foreign words.

"Is goot to hear the language of the homeland!" Jacob Franck declared. "Now the long journey is vorth the troubles."

Miguel wondered how these guttural noises could ever sound good to anyone's ears. When his family spoke Spanish, the words were as fluid as water rushing over a smooth rock. Now that he was going to school, he thought that even the new English words he was learning had a soft, rolling sound that tumbled out easily.

Doc Meyer saw the look on Miguel's face and mistook it for disbelief. "You are too young to understand what it is to leave everything you have known and come to a place where no one speaks even your language." He patted Miguel's head as if he were a puppy. "Bless God, you should never know, *Miguelito*."

"Amen," his mother agreed. "May we always be together in this new country." Mamá had put on a fresh dress, and filigreed silver combs held her hair in place.

"Yes," said Papá, "a country that keeps changing around us!"

"At least our food hasn't changed!" Mamá said with a smile. "Please come and eat." She gestured to the dining room, and everyone filed in.

Miguel stood behind his chair, as did the others, until his parents were seated. Then each person sat at the long wooden table, its thick legs carved with spiral designs. Miguel's hands brushed against the familiar white tablecloth, its faded embroidered flowers curling over the edges. Every Friday night Mamá set out the same cloth, and every Monday she washed it, hanging it to bleach in the Arizona sun. Before her were two silver candlesticks, which she polished to a shine every Friday morning. They looked elegant in spite of a few dents and scratches.

"These candlesticks came from Spain more than three hundred years ago," Papá said with a note of pride in his voice. He flapped open his napkin with a flourish and settled it onto his lap. Miguel knew this was the opening for Papá to tell the family story once again. He knew it by heart, in Papá's exact words, but didn't dare interrupt. "Traditionally, these candlesticks were handed down to the . . ."

. . . *oldest daughter in each generation.* Miguel finished the sentence in his head. He imagined all the Abrano mothers who came before his, as if they were lined up one behind the other lighting candles in the very same candlesticks. What a long history they had. He wondered what stories the candlesticks would tell if only they could speak. Still, he didn't see why Doc Meyer and the peddler would be interested in family stories.

"Since I had no sisters," Papá continued, "my mother chose to give them to Elena." He beamed at his wife. "Now we have three sons! What to do?"

"Perhaps when you get married, Esteban," Mamá said, "we will pass them on to your wife." She gave him an encouraging glance. "Maybe soon?"

Esteban nearly choked. "Married?" he gasped. "These candleholders are safe with you for a long time to come, Mamá."

"I hope it's not too much longer, *mijo*," she said. "I have waited long enough for a daughter!" Mamá stood as Carmella brought a lit taper from the kitchen. As Mamá lit the thick white candles, shadows and light danced across her face.

"Lighting candles reminds me of my own mother," Señor Franck said hesitantly. "Each Friday at sundown, she marked the start of the Sabbath with a prayer over the candle flames."

"I had forgotten that Israelites observe the Sabbath on Saturday, and not Sunday," Doc Meyer commented. "Different bibles, different calendar."

Mamá turned to Señor Franck. "Perhaps you would like to recite your traditional prayer over the candles?"

The peddler fidgeted with his tie and humbly asked, "If it vould not offend you, Don Mateo, maybe you permit me to recite the Hebrew blessing offering thanks for the day of rest? I think is goot for Saturday or Sunday." He looked around the table and added quickly. "It vould please me to share this, but only if you wish it."

"Please, Señor," Mamá encouraged him. "It would make the evening special for us."

Miguel was about to protest when his father gave him a withering glance. He shrank into his chair as if trying to avoid his father's displeasure as well as the peddler's words.

Señor Franck stood and held his hands on either side of the glowing candles. "Of course, this prayer is for the Mamá in the house to say," he explained, "but even though it is only me, I think God listens anyway." He made a circular motion with his hands, stroking the air as if he were coaxing the light toward his face. Miguel squirmed in his chair. Was this a heathen ritual, calling up some power from the flames? He searched his father's face for an answer as the peddler chanted words Miguel couldn't understand. In spite of a sing-song rhythm, Hebrew sounded even worse to his ears than German, and more frightening.

Papá's eyes were closed, as if he were making a prayer of his own. How could his father remain so calm? As Miguel stared at him, Papá's eyes blinked open and he nodded at Miguel. The peddler's strange words hung in the air, and Miguel wished he could chase them from the house.

"What about *our* blessing?" he prompted.

"Of course," Papá said quickly, as if he had been jolted awake. With hands folded, he bowed his head and mumbled a blessing over the food they were about to eat.

"Amen," Miguel said firmly and made the sign of the cross. His parents and brothers followed.

"So now we toast!" Doc Meyer declared, breaking the solemn mood. He lifted his glass of wine and waved it in the direction of the others, as they, too, lifted their glasses. "Here's to the future state of Arizona and all her new citizens!" Miguel held up his glass of lemonade, but didn't take as much as a sip. If new citizens included people like the Jewish peddler with his heathen prayers, Miguel hoped that Arizona wouldn't be quite so welcoming.

"And now the bread," Papá said eagerly. "My favorite." He reached for the shiny, braided loaf that replaced the flat flour tortillas the family usually ate each night. "Elena bakes this herself. It's my mother's recipe, also handed down for generations." As Carmella came in carrying a covered casserole, Papá winked and said in a fake whisper, "The secret is that it's made with eggs, but we don't even share this with Carmella!"

"*Bien*, Don Mateo," Carmella teased. "Doña

Elena gives me enough work. She can make this bread whenever she wishes." She set the dish in the center of the table. Hot steam from the food formed beads of water that slipped down onto the clay platter beneath the serving bowl.

The yeasty smell of the warm loaf softened Miguel's concerns. He looked around the table at his family. They were together as they were each Friday night, sharing a festive meal. It was like a holiday. Although he often complained about how strict his mother was, allowing no excuses for missing this dinner each week, Miguel felt a secret pleasure in the tradition. He took a bite of the sweet bread. In spite of the stranger at their table, nothing had really changed.

But tonight Miguel would try to change one thing—Papá's rule about riding alone. He stared into the light of the candle flames and felt a glimmer of hope. His father was enjoying the meal and the company. He was in a jovial mood. It was the perfect time to ask.

Jacob Franck's eyes grew wide as Mamá lifted the casserole lid to reveal plump chicken pieces nestled on a bed of rice laced with tomatoes, onions, and peppers.

"I thank you for your generous hospitality," he declared. "Outside my village in Germany, no Jews are velcome. That is why I come to America. Not everyone treats a stranger like me kindly, but even alone in the desert, it feels safer . . ."

"Being alone is not as dangerous as people around here think," Miguel said. "Don't you agree, Señor Franck?"

"I have never been frightened," the peddler said, cutting into his chicken. "A little nervous sometimes, I confess, but I just keep the eyes open and go about my business. So far, all is safe."

"*Exactamente!*" Miguel exclaimed. He cleared his throat. "Papá," he began, "you know what a good rider I am, so . . ."

"Speaking of riders," Ruben interrupted, "some are not so safe." Miguel glared at his brother. He had been ready to ask his father about riding into town on his own, and now Ruben had spoiled the perfect opportunity. Ruben kept talking, ignoring Miguel. "In town, you're in danger if someone thinks you cheated at cards. In the desert, a bandit could steal your horse and shoot you without a second thought."

Esteban winked at his brother mischievously.

"Now we hear it's not even safe to walk along Main Street. Seems some people race their buggies through town."

Doc Meyer held his fork and knife over the plate, and responded with a laugh. "I admit it! The apothecary was speeding wit' the buggy. So I bring myself to court and give myself a fair trial."

"But you're the justice of the peace too!" Ruben snorted. "How could it be a fair trial?" Jacob Franck chuckled at the revelation, his string tie bobbing against his collar.

"Sure it was fair," Doc Meyer insisted. "I declare myself guilty and fine myself five dollars."

"You truly have brought law and order to Tucson," Papá said with a sly smile.

Miguel didn't laugh. His brother had ruined the chance to change his father's mind about riding alone. He ate glumly as the men started talking about politics. They expressed their anger at the United States government refusing to make Arizona Territory a state, and then joked and laughed as the peddler shared stories of his adventures.

Mamá lit the oil lamps in the parlor after dinner, and the group settled into the soft leather chairs arranged around the fireplace. The grate was black and empty since there was no need for a fire in the warmth that still lingered in the evening air.

Just as Miguel found another opportunity to spring his question, Papá addressed the peddler. "Can you read Hebrew, Señor Franck?"

"Yah, sure," he said. "I learned for my bar mitzvah. A prayer book I have, and I am reading when I am alone in my travels. It keeps me company and keeps me from forgetting."

Papá looked questioningly toward Mamá, and Miguel caught her almost imperceptible nod of approval.

"In that case, I have something I'd like to share with you," Papá said hesitantly. "And it involves a small favor." Taking a key from the pocket of his embroidered vest, Papá unlocked a drawer in the sideboard and removed a cracked, leather-bound book that Miguel had never seen before. Why was it hidden?

CHAPTER 4
A Startling Revelation

"This diary was written by the first Abrano who arrived here from Spain," Papá said solemnly. "Some bits of our background have been passed down, but there is so much we don't know."

"Before Don Mateo and I married," Mamá said, "he told me what he had heard from his father. We discovered that we share a similar history." She nodded to the book. "No one has ever been able to read this diary, and Mateo has always wished to hear his ancestor's words."

Papá took a deep breath. "You see, although we knew fragments of our background, we never discussed it outside our own family. We weren't sure how our neighbors—and even our friends—would feel about us if they knew. People in the territory speak often of accepting all settlers, but they don't always act accordingly."

Like Berto's stories about Israelites with horns, Miguel mused. *And the sign on the door of his family's café.*

Papá rested his hand on Doc Meyer's shoulder. "I trust that anything you hear tonight will find an open heart."

"Between goot friends, there should always be honesty," Doc Meyer said. "Nothing can change our friendship."

Papá addressed Señor Franck. "You can help us hear the family story if you can read this diary," he said.

Miguel didn't understand. "Why didn't you read the book yourself, Papá?" Why was his father bringing the book out now?

"There is more to know than the fact that the first Abrano came from Spain with the conquistadors," Papá answered. He addressed the peddler. "The difficulty for us is that the diary is written in Hebrew. Do you think you can help?"

"Why isn't it written in Spanish?" Miguel asked uncertainly.

Papá cleared his throat and looked steadily at Miguel. "The answer isn't so simple, *mijo,* but if you will be patient, you will begin to understand. Tonight, you begin your real education as an Abrano." His father emphasized the family name, speaking it with a fierce pride.

"We shared the little that we know with Esteban and Ruben when they were just your age," Mamá said. "Your father was waiting for the right time to explain it to you too."

Papá hesitated, then said, "You are about to turn thirteen, Miguel, and it is time for us to usher you into manhood. That is one more tradition that has been handed down for generations. If Señor Franck can read this diary, we will all learn more than we ever knew. Once we hear it, perhaps you will realize why I have told you that becoming a priest might not be the right path for you."

Jacob Franck wiped his hands against his black pants and reached for the book. For a moment, it seemed suspended between the two men. Miguel thought he saw a flicker of uncertainty in his father's eyes before he released his hold. The peddler opened the back cover with reverence, and a ragged bit of dried leather fell from the cracked binding onto the floor.

Miguel leaned down to pick it up, and as he did,

he caught a glimpse of a page of neatly written markings. The black ink was still dark and shiny against the yellowed page. The strange writing was unlike anything Miguel had ever seen. How could these lines form words? He suspected that Señor Franck couldn't read them either, since he had opened the book backwards, starting with the last page.

The peddler moved closer to the circle of light formed by the oil lamp and squinted. His lips moved silently. Gingerly, he turned the page and scanned it. His dark eyes widened. "I heard of this writing, but never did I see it," he murmured. "This is *the code*." He looked searchingly at Papá.

"The code?" Papá echoed. "What do you mean?"

"Hundreds of years ago," the visitor said, "the Catholic Church forbade all the Jews of Spain from practicing their religion. Thousands left to make new lives in other lands, but many stayed in their homes by pretending to convert. This they were forced to do or risk torture and death at the hands of the Inquisition, dreaded judges of the church. Even in the face of such danger, many secretly kept their Jewish traditions." He sat straighter in the chair. "Such courage they showed!"

Pretending to be Catholic isn't an act of courage, Miguel

thought dismissively. Father Ignacio despaired of the Papagos who kept their heathen practices even after accepting the church. Were there also Israelites who only pretended to believe?

The peddler pointed to the open page. "These secret Jews, they make a code that no outsider can figure out. Like their Bible, the pages go from back to front, and the vords they read from right to left. The letters are from the Hebrew alphabet, but if you know how to pronounce each word out loud, the language you hear is Spanish! If enemies discover any of these writings, how can they guess what it says?" He smiled his crooked smile. "Smart, yah?" The group murmured its agreement, waiting to hear more.

"Maybe those Israelites had a clever code," Miguel said impatiently, "but what does it have to do with us?"

"Listen," Papá admonished him with a stern look. "You have asked to be treated like a man and not a child. You think that having a birthday means that you should ride wherever you please on your own." Papá's voice rose. "To be a man has nothing to do with privileges. To be an Abrano—you must understand where you came from."

"If only my family had such a book," Mamá said. "It is a *milagro*—a miracle—to hear the voice of your ancestor."

Jacob Franck glanced from Miguel's parents and brothers to Miguel. "This ancestor of yours had a powerful name—Aharon ben Avraham. The man who wrote this diary, in English he has the biblical name Aaron, son of Abraham."

Now Miguel was certain that the diary had nothing to do with his family. The person who wrote it wasn't even an Abrano. So why did Papá want to hear the secret words in this crumbling book?

Ruben sat straighter in his chair. "Señor Franck, can you read it for us?"

"My Spanish is not so goot," he apologized. "Maybe a little we can read tonight. Then tomorrow your Papá and I, together ve figure this out."

"There is so much more I wish to ask you," Papá said. "There are so many family traditions, like our Friday night meal and baking the braided bread, which we learned from our parents and our grandparents. But like the blessing over the candles that none remembered, there is so much that has been lost. When you recited the blessing over the candles tonight, it was the first time we had ever heard it."

The peddler nodded, and then settled back and began to read aloud in a halting voice. His finger pointed to each word on the brittle page, and he stopped occasionally to let Papá correct or explain an unfamiliar Spanish word. The room was hushed, except for the raspy breathing of Jacob Franck as he stumbled through the lines of mysterious writing.

To all who follow in my sad footsteps, this is the true account of Aharon ben Avraham, begun this fifteenth day of September in the year 1546. Although my family was forced to be baptized in the Catholic Church more than fifty years ago, and our names changed to hide our background, we were among those who kept our Jewish beliefs hidden. Called *conversos*, we never escaped the suspicions of the Inquisition, and lived in constant fear for our very lives.

Papá sat with his chin resting in his hand, concentrating on the halting words.

After I had a family of my own, I decided that we must free ourselves from our secret life.

With a melancholy heart, I gathered my loving wife, Joya, and our seven children, along with a few of our most precious belongings. We turned our backs on the city of our ancestors.

Miguel tapped his fingers impatiently against the arm of his chair. Why must he listen to this strange tale? Mamá scowled at him, and he folded his hands to keep them still.

The peddler kept reading, stopping and starting again with Papá's help.

After one full day of travel, when our escape was at hand, soldiers of the Inquisition overtook us. With only a small dagger to protect my dearest ones, I was quickly captured. The soldiers bound me hand and foot, and as I struggled against my bonds, they mercilessly killed my beloved Joya and each of my adored children. The soldiers shouted, *Traitors! Heathens!* As for me, I wept and cried, *Murderers!*

I was beaten senseless while my family's blood soaked the earth of their homeland. When I next opened my bruised and swollen eyes to the horror of what I had lost, I was shackled on a musty ship heading to the far shores of New Spain, conscripted into the service of the king's conquistadors. I could not fight my captors but, instead, would be forced to fight for them in an uncivilized land.

Even with no fire burning in the grate and the air turning chill, Miguel felt as if he were suffocating. He couldn't bear to hear another word, but the peddler kept translating haltingly, and somehow Miguel felt as if he were a captive of each horrifying word. Everyone in the room seemed gripped by the spell cast by the flowery and emotional words of Aharon ben Avraham.

The only possessions left were my wife's silver candlesticks, tucked clumsily into my tall leather boots. The memory of Joya's face as she lit the Sabbath candles became my strength. I grasped for the image of the flickering light and made it my will to live. I vowed to continue our traditions in the barren land around me, to honor the memory of my family.

Miguel felt a sudden jolt of recognition. Were the candlesticks in the diary the same ones that stood on his family's table each Friday night? Surely, that couldn't be! There was no time to sort out the thoughts that crowded his head as he was drawn to the peddler's voice like a moth caught in a flickering lantern.

I continued to use the name Alejandro Abrano and learned to be a soldier. I despised every waking hour, forced to fight against the native people who were so like me in too many ways. The Inquisition robbed them of their religion, their land, and their lives, just as I had lost my homeland and my family. The survivors were compelled to accept the church's teachings and abandon or hide their true beliefs. Many days I prayed for death to end my hateful life, but God did not answer my prayers. In time, my talents in navigation allowed me to lay my sword aside. Instead of fighting as a soldier, I was named map-maker. Within these pages, I will record how I earned honor in the service of the very king who destroyed my life. In time, God blessed me with a new wife and healthy children. Together, we have preserved some few traditions. May my children and grandchildren, and every generation of Abranos, know this story and honor the remnants of our past.

Abrano! The mapmaker's name had been changed by his own ancestors! Miguel's ears burned with shame. How could Papá have betrayed the family in front of strangers? He glared at his father. Surely, this was all a misunderstanding. Abranos had always been faithful Catholics—hadn't they?

Esteban and Ruben looked steadily at Miguel, and he felt that his brothers had betrayed him too. "Has everyone in the family heard this story before?" he demanded. "Everyone except me?" Miguel stood uncertainly, his legs feeling as if they might buckle beneath him. "It's not true," he snapped, waiting— hoping—for someone to erase this moment.

"I've upset you," Papá said quickly, his voice soft. "That wasn't what I wanted." He held Miguel with a disappointed look. "I had planned to tell you the story next week when you turned thirteen, but this opportunity came up suddenly. I couldn't let it pass." He placed his hand over Miguel's, and every muscle in Miguel's body froze. "This book truly is written by the first of our family to come to New Spain," Papá said evenly, "a secret Jew. He was given this land in return for his service to the king. We owe him our lives, and we must listen to his voice."

Miguel pulled his hand away, his breath coming in quick gasps. "I am Catholic," he breathed, almost to himself. "Father Ignacio said I might have a calling to the priesthood." Miguel had hoped for a sign from God to tell him if that was the path he was meant to follow. He shivered. *Is this the sign?*

"We were baptized Catholics, *mijo*," Papá reassured him, "but we cannot let our heritage die. We wish to reclaim it, if only to honor those who came before us. Our heritage is part of us—part of you."

Mamá's forehead was furrowed with concern. Quietly she said, "I have always felt blessed to have found your father, and to share our Jewish backgrounds. We understand each other, and believe in what we must do. That is why we have told you the story and told it to your brothers."

Mamá continued in her gentle voice. "Just as our ancestors welcomed the Sabbath on Friday nights, I willingly light the candles and bake the braided bread. Abranos haven't known the Hebrew blessings for generations, but I would never let the tradition die. Perhaps, as we learn more, we will embrace this lost heritage. However small our knowledge, you must carry on the traditions, as well."

Miguel looked from the wooden crucifix that hung on the wall to the face of the peddler, with his scruffy beard. Shock and humiliation washed over him, and he felt his breath coming in great gulps. "It's not true!" he declared. "No one in my family was ever an Israelite!"

Mamá rose from her chair and stretched out her arms. "Ah, *Miguelito*, you were not ready."

Miguel's anger mixed with hot tears that streaked his face. With everyone's eyes fixed on him, he was overcome with shame. He turned and rushed into the kitchen.

Carmella looked up in alarm, the dish she was washing slipping into the dishpan. "*¿Qué pasa?*" she exclaimed. "What happened?"

Miguel bolted out the door. In the comfort of darkness, he raced toward the corral.

"*¿Quién pasa?*" called a ranch hand, posted as a guard. "Who's there?"

Miguel choked out a reply. "*Yo soy Miguel!*" Behind him, he heard the dull thud of his brothers' boots on the packed ground. His fingers fumbled to untie the reins of a saddle horse hitched at the railing. He mounted and raced off, kicking the horse's flanks harder than he ever had before. His brothers' shouts echoed in his ears.

"*Miguelito!* Come back!" Their calls were swept away like the air that flew past Miguel as he rode. He couldn't face Doc Meyer or the raggedy peddler. Not Mamá or Papá or his brothers. He couldn't go back. Finally, he would ride across the desert alone.

CHAPTER 5
A Desert Ride

Miguel urged the horse faster, keeping pace with his galloping heartbeat. He had to get away from his family's shocking secrets, away from the diary's awful tale. Pale moonlight outlined the dark shapes of boulders and cactus, and the horse changed direction often to avoid obstacles in its path.

Miguel bent low over the horse's neck, racing forward blindly until his head was emptied of all thoughts. He sensed only the deepening chill of the spring night and the feeling that he and the horse were one, whispering across the desert like the wind.

The horse's panting disturbed the silence that engulfed him. Miguel rubbed his hand along the back of the animal's neck, and frothy sweat slicked against his skin. He slowed to a trot, fearing the horse would collapse from exhaustion. He could tell by its swayed back that it was an old mount. *Papá would never forgive me for deliberately pushing a horse too hard.*

Miguel looked for a place to rest. The horse shuddered, its belly heaving between Miguel's legs. He jerked the reins to the left and headed for a stand of cottonwood trees silhouetted against the starry sky. He didn't remember a grove like this near the ranch. If there were cottonwoods, there was probably water too.

How far had he come? *I don't even know which direction I rode*, Miguel realized. The horse had taken many turns, and he hadn't noted any passing landmarks to help guide his way back.

The cottonwoods offered a welcoming shelter. Like the horse, Miguel was panting from the exertion of the ride. Vapor formed as their warm breath hit the air. With the sun gone, the desert was quickly growing cold. Miguel loosened his grip on the reins and slid onto the sandy soil, but the horse shied away.

"Whoa, there," Miguel said softly. He stroked the horse's long nose, as she snorted and pulled back. The sour odor of cat urine drifted in the air. Now Miguel understood the horse's nervousness. A puma had visited the stream not long before and marked its territory. He hoped the big cat was not lurking in the trees. He stood still, listening for any sound, but heard only the faint rippling of a brook.

Miguel led the horse to the water, and it lowered its head to drink from the shallow stream. Miguel knelt down, holding tightly to the reins, and cupped his hand into the cold water. His hair fell toward his face as he sipped the water that trickled through his fingers. *I've forgotten my hat*, he thought with regret. He had rushed from the house without thinking. Besides protecting him, the hat would have made a useful cup.

Miguel heard a faint rustle in the scrubby bushes at the far edge of the cottonwoods. He groped along the stream bank until he found a willowy branch. If a puma was lurking in the brush, he might be able to frighten it away. He whipped the branch against a tree, and the sound cut through the air. Miguel blinked into the darkness, alert to danger. He thought he heard the sound of low breathing, and tried to peer into the underbrush.

I probably heard my own breathing or the panting of the horse, he reassured himself. Maybe the earlier noise was just a burrowing pack rat. *Or was it a mountain lion, ready to spring?* A shiver of fear spread down the back of his neck.

Miguel knew the horse's energy was spent. It tossed its head and pawed the ground. Miguel couldn't seem to calm it, but he would have to stay where he was for the night, no matter what other creature might be hidden nearby. He wasn't likely to find another sheltered spot.

As soon as the sun rose in the morning, he would look for the Santa Catalina Mountains. The ranch was just southeast of the tallest peak. Miguel's brothers would think their *Miguelito* needed an escort. If he could just get home before they headed out to search for him, they would see that he was old enough to take care of himself. He made up his mind to start before dawn.

A snapping twig made Miguel jump. He whacked the branch against the ground, but only succeeded in scaring the horse, which gave a whimpering whinny.

If there's a rifle in the saddlebags, I can shoot if I have to. He doubted he could hit a moving puma, but even the sound of a rifle shot might be enough to scare it off.

He rummaged through the saddlebags, pulling out a pack of playing cards tied with twine, and then a medicine pouch with vials of powders and rolls of white bandages. *This must be Doc Meyer's mare,* Miguel realized. He searched his memory for her name . . . Zuzi! That was it!

"Easy, Zuzi," he murmured, and the jittery horse turned her head as if she recognized her name. "It's going to be all right."

Miguel was sorry he had taken Charlie Meyer's mare. The apothecary would be worried about her, and probably angry that Miguel had been so thoughtless. Surely, Papá would give Doc Meyer another mount to ride home, and Miguel would return Zuzi in the morning. Hadn't the apothecary said that his horse knew the way home, even if he rode her while he was asleep? All Miguel would have to do is let her lead the way.

He continued to search the bags, pulling out a leather hobble that he slipped over the horse's forelegs. The soft loops would keep her from running off in the night without being tied up. Miguel foraged in the saddlebag again and discovered a horn-handled jackknife. The small blade wasn't as much protection as a rifle, but it could be useful if he needed to defend himself. He dropped the knife into his left pocket. He uncinched the saddle and rubbed the horse dry with the saddle blanket, talking in soft tones. Next, he slid the harness over Zuzi's ears, which twitched alertly, and slipped the bit from her mouth. There was little to graze on, but at least the water would hold her overnight.

"I promise you a bucket of the best feed on the ranch, girl," he whispered. "*Mañana*—tomorrow— as soon as we get home."

Thoughts of Miguel's family came rushing back. He would soon have to face Papá's anger and the shame of what he had done. Running away had been childish, just when he wanted to be treated like a man. Papá had kept the Abranos' secret hidden so long. Why had he told Miguel at all? Bitterness rose in his throat. His life could never be the same now that he knew his ancestors were Israelites. If only he could wipe the memory away and stop feeling its nagging ache.

Under the shelter of the trees, Miguel wrapped himself in the blanket. It was damp with the horse's sweat, but he was too cold to be fussy. As he fought an overwhelming tiredness to stay alert, the night's events played out in his mind like a recurring dream. *It doesn't matter about some dead ancestor*, he thought. *That doesn't make me any different.*

Would the church still consider him a true Catholic? He would have to tell Father Ignacio the whole story and listen to the priest's decision. Miguel fought against tears, folding his arms tightly across his chest.

As hard as he tried, his eyes kept closing, and he dozed for minutes at a time before jerking awake. Suddenly, Zuzi whinnied in alarm. Miguel leaped to his feet. A sharp pinging sound screamed through the air as an arrow flew past Miguel's shoulder and lodged in a tree with a loud *thwack*!

Indians! Miguel raced to the horse and began pulling at the hobble. His hands fumbled with the loops as Zuzi shied backward. *Hurry!* he urged himself. *Faster!* He never should have hobbled the horse, or removed her harness. He should have been ready to ride at the slightest sign of danger.

Stepping from behind the trees, a band of warriors appeared like apparitions in the night. Miguel froze at the twang of their bowstrings pulling taut. Even in the darkness he could see the arrows pointed at his chest. A hand gripped his arm, and Miguel struggled to pull free.

The rustling Miguel had heard had been the warriors, not a puma. If only he'd paid attention to Zuzi's skittishness, he might have ridden away in time.

In a flash, he thought of the jackknife in his pocket, but what use was such a small weapon against a band of armed men? Like in the journal's story of Aharon ben Avraham, who was defenseless against the soldiers of the Inquisition, one small knife was useless.

The warrior who held him pointed at Miguel's boots. "Give!" he commanded.

Miguel stared into the stony face of the man towering over him. A clutch of feathered arrows protruded from a beaded leather case slung across his back. It was different from any quiver Miguel had ever seen, with two cases joined together and long fringes flowing from its edge.

He was paralyzed with fear. Without warning, the Indian cuffed Miguel sharply across the ear. The man's long black hair moved in time with the blow, swinging beneath a white headband. Miguel fell backward, and the horse blanket dropped to the ground.

"Give!" the warrior repeated more gruffly. He kicked at the leather boots. Miguel's face and ear stung, and he didn't wait to be hit again. He pulled off his boots and handed them up. The men sur-rounding him wore tall leather moccasins. The tops were folded over below the knees. The only other clothing they wore was a cotton breechcloth wound between their legs and hanging in long folds from their waists.

Sweat beaded on Miguel's forehead in spite of the chill. He remembered which tribe wore such distinctive moccasins and carried double quivers. "Apache," he breathed.

"No Apache!" sneered the warrior as he tugged Miguel's boots on in place of his moccasins. "We are Indé!" The other members of the band kept their arrows trained on Miguel. They stood silently as their companion strode off into the shadows, dig-ging his booted feet into the soft earth.

A second Indian pulled the hobble from Doc Meyer's horse and tossed it into the brush. He mounted the horse bareback and rode in a different direction than his companion had walked. Miguel had always believed he could outride any attackers, but now he had no horse. A cold fear settled in the pit of his stomach.

Miguel didn't think he'd ever heard of a tribe called Indé. If these warriors weren't Apache, maybe they would be satisfied with taking his horse and his boots. *It will take me longer, but I can walk home, even if I have to do it in my socks*, he consoled himself. *If only they let me go.*

The half light of dawn began to lighten the sky. Miguel shivered and wondered how the warriors surrounding him could travel with bare chests. Didn't they feel the icy chill?

They lowered their bows and returned their arrows to their quivers. Then the band formed a line. The leader at the front picked up the horse blanket and after examining it admiringly, draped it around his shoulders like a trophy. Miguel felt grateful that he still had his shirt. *Maybe now they'll leave me*, he thought hopefully.

The leader roughly pulled Miguel to his feet and pushed him into the middle of the line. He pointed in a different direction than the paths taken by the two warriors who had stolen Miguel's horse and his boots.

"Walk," a slim muscular Indian behind him ordered. This time, Miguel obeyed immediately, struggling to keep up with the swift pace.

"Where are you taking me?" he asked. His question hung in the air, unanswered. Miguel watched the narrow path in front of him. He didn't want to tread on a prowling rattlesnake without his boots for protection. He turned his head to the warrior behind him. "Where are we going?"

"No talk!" the young man growled. Miguel marched forward, walking into the desert on an unknown trail.

CHAPTER 6
A Grueling March

The horizon glowed red, and Miguel watched flaming rays of sun reach into the desert sky. *I've got to remember that the rising sun is on my right*, he thought. *That means we're walking north.* He looked at the mountains that loomed in the distance. He had to remember the way back in case there was any chance of escape.

Miguel's socks snagged against the rough stones underfoot, and he was breathless from walking so fast. Yet his captors seemed to exert no energy at all, moving along without slackening their pace. Whenever Miguel slowed, he was shoved from behind. He kept looking for the warrior who had left wearing his boots, but the man hadn't returned. *I'd be able to walk faster with my boots on*, he complained silently.

The sun rose overhead, heat shimmered up from the desert, and still Miguel was forced on. The shivers that had slipped up his spine during the night turned to rivers of sweat that rolled between his shoulders and soaked his shirt in the glaring midday heat.

When the sun became oppressive, the band walked in the shade of rocky outcroppings and occasionally stopped for a drink. Miguel was amazed that the men seemed to know exactly where to find a pool or a trickle of water. Now they climbed through a cluster of boulders and gathered around a shallow depression filled with clear water. Miguel was mystified. Did they often travel the same path, knowing the water was there, or had they just discovered it for the first time?

Each Indé scooped a gourdful of water, and he watched them drink while his own mouth stayed parched. They filled their gourds a second time and added a dry powder from their leather pouches. It looked like the cornmeal Carmella ground and stored in a clay jar. Miguel watched hungrily as the warriors stirred the mixture with their fingers and scooped it into their mouths.

He hadn't eaten anything since last night's dinner. The memory of Mamá's Friday night meal sent pangs of hunger through his stomach, and feelings of remorse through his head.

Only after the warriors had eaten did they seem to remember Miguel's presence. The line leader handed him a dipper and motioned to the water hole. Miguel filled the gourd and drank, feeling the icy mountain water wet his dry lips and throat. He dipped again, but before he could drink, the leader put his hand across the top of the gourd.

"*Pinole*," he said, pouring some grain into the gourd. He made a stirring motion in the air with his fingers, and Miguel copied what the others had done. The loose mixture was gritty, but more filling than he expected.

Just when Miguel thought he would have a chance to rest, the line formed again and he was marched into the low foothills. Once he stumbled on some loose rocks and fell forward. Immediately, the warrior at his back pulled him to his feet and pushed him along at the same relentless pace. Miguel searched the man's eyes for any sign of kindness, but the chiseled face before him was as expressionless as a stone.

Two warriors ahead of Miguel spoke briefly in their own language. Although Miguel was surrounded, he had never felt more alone.

The band traveled higher into the foothills, following a rough trail that wound between large rock formations. Miguel would never have realized there was a path if he had been on his own. He was traveling farther and farther from home with no way to escape.

Now Miguel hoped that his brothers and Papá had organized a search party that might rescue him. His mind swirled with thoughts of other ranchers who had been captured, always by Apache. The men of Tucson would gather quietly in the center of town and form a posse to ride off and search. They alerted the cavalry at Fort Lowell, and mounted soldiers joined the hunt. Sometimes the rescue party succeeded. More often, they brought home a bloodied body draped across a pack mule.

Miguel's sense of helplessness deepened. *How could anyone search for me? No one knows about the cottonwood trees, or even that I've been captured. How would they know which direction I rode?* Even Miguel couldn't say which way he had gone or how he had ended up at the stream.

A rough push from behind forced Miguel to focus on the trail in front of him. As if he were a horse prodded with sharp spurs, he trotted ahead in spite of the heat and his thirst, in spite of the stones that cut through his socks and bit into his skin. Soon shadows lengthened in the fading afternoon light. Not even the whistle of a bird broke the silence. Then, like a rock dropped into a well, the sun fell below the mountain.

Miguel was overcome with exhaustion. *Maybe it would be better to be killed than take one more step,* he thought. Just then, the band entered a clearing bordered by overhanging boulders. A campfire glowed beneath the shelter, and five warriors sat cooking shanks of meat. Miguel blinked, wondering if this was all a mirage.

The warriors greeted one another with words that sounded more foreign than the German greetings Doc Meyer and the peddler had exchanged, and less understandable than the prayer Jacob Franck had chanted. He sank onto a flat rock, his socks stained with blood from his cut feet. A young Indé with a faint scar on his neck strode through the camp, and Miguel immediately recognized the man who had stolen his boots. The thief fixed a cold stare at Miguel and turned away. He had taken a different path, yet ended up at the campsite before Miguel and the band that had led him there.

He's wearing moccasins again, Miguel realized. *What has he done with my boots?*

The band relaxed around the fire. None seemed tired from the long hike, and none seemed to fear discovery by a search party.

Miguel had begun to distinguish between the different men and had given each one a name that reminded him of their different attitudes. In his thoughts, he named the warrior who walked behind him and prodded him along the trail as Stone Face. Now Stone Face handed Miguel a gourd of water, and he gratefully gulped it down. His thirst was unbearable, his throat choked with dust.

Miguel chose a name for the Indé man who had taken his boots and returned without them— Bootless Warrior. The thief approached Miguel with a second dipper of water, and Miguel eyed him with suspicion. He reached cautiously for the gourd, but Bootless Warrior tipped out its contents, pouring water over Miguel's raw, bloodied feet. A thin smile crossed his lips as Miguel gasped at the stinging pain.

The man pounded his fist against his bare chest. "Indé strong!" he taunted Miguel.

The insult stung as much as the water that

ran over Miguel's cut flesh. He didn't need to be reminded that the warriors were stronger than he was. *How long will they hold me before they decide I'm slowing them down too much?* If he couldn't keep up, they would surely kill him. Gingerly, he peeled off the wet, shredded socks and tossed them aside. They hadn't protected him on the march and weren't of any use.

One of the men stepped closer and spoke to Bootless Warrior. Miguel couldn't tell where one word ended and another began. The sounds grated like stones rumbling down a mountain.

But Bootless Warrior understood perfectly. He tugged the front of Miguel's shirt. "Give!" he commanded. Miguel didn't want to lose his shirt, but he knew it was useless—and dangerous—to refuse. He pulled the shirt over his head, feeling the cold night air creeping up his arms and chest. A few more warriors gathered around, fingering the cotton fabric and admiring the tiny gold stars that dotted the midnight blue cloth. Then Miguel watched helplessly as Bootless Warrior sliced it with a sharp stone and distributed the strips to his companions. With a snorting laugh, he tossed the detached sleeves at Miguel's feet.

Miguel seized the remnants and wrapped them tightly around his cut feet. Like his shredded socks, the cotton bindings wouldn't last long. He edged closer to the fire, hugging his arms around his bare back.

Fat sizzled into the flames, and an unfamiliar odor rose from the cooking meat. Miguel's stomach rumbled its hunger. He and his captors had eaten almost nothing all day. The warrior who led the group adjusted the horse blanket around his shoulders. Miguel thought of him as Line Leader. He leaned forward and handed Miguel a bone, thick with blackened meat. The smell was repulsive, but Miguel's gnawing hunger overcame his reluctance. Without food, he would surely die.

Bootless Warrior glared as Miguel chewed at the tough, sinewy meat. What animal was it from? His captor seemed to guess Miguel's question. He pointed behind some jagged boulders, and Miguel turned to see a large carcass, its bones sticking out helter-skelter. A leather saddle was tossed to the side. With horror, Miguel recognized the remains of Charlie Meyer's horse. His stomach roiled. Was he eating Zuzi?

A wave of nausea rose into Miguel's throat. Dropping the bone as if it were a live snake, he fell to his knees, retching into the sand. Through the pounding pulse in his ears, he heard the derisive laughter of his captors. Bootless Warrior, Line Leader, and Stone Face sneered.

Every muscle in Miguel's body ached, and his stomach gurgled its emptiness. He crawled to a patch of sand surrounded by boulders and curled up as tightly as a fist. He fell into a fitful sleep filled with shadowy images of riderless horses galloping across the desert.

CHAPTER 7
The Cry of the Owl

Days passed, and each one brought new challenges. Now Miguel inched blindly up a rock face, groping for small crevices to use as toe and finger holds. His shoulders cramped with the effort, and he feared he would drop onto the trail below. He tried not to look up at Bootless Warrior and his companions who peered over the ledge above him, judging his progress.

Miguel sensed Bootless Warrior's withering stare. Below, thorny cactus sprouted from narrow cracks and stunted bushes twisted toward the light. The desert floor was far below him, and Miguel's head reeled when he realized how high he was as he clung to the rocks. He forced himself to focus on the next place where he might find a grip.

Pull, he told himself, forcing himself a few inches higher. His bare chest rubbed against the cold stones, but perspiration beaded on his forehead. Reaching the top only meant more marching, but losing his hold meant certain death. He tightened his fingers. *Pull!*

For the past three days, Miguel had followed the mountain trail relentlessly from dawn until nightfall. Today, when the trail ended at the rock face, the warriors in front of him had scaled the sheer cliff as if they were scrambling across a flat spit of sand.

Miguel was constantly surprised by their skills. Now he understood why the cavalry had so much trouble tracking down raiders. Each of the warriors in this band could walk swiftly for ten or twelve hours without slowing. They wound between rocks and through prickly underbrush following paths that no soldier would ever notice and no horse could travel.

It seemed that just when Miguel thought he would collapse without a drink to revive him, the band came to a water hole. One afternoon they filled their gourds from a steady drip inside a shallow cave. They ate little, but there was always something to stanch their hunger. Besides pieces of dried horse-meat, which Miguel refused, the men collected roots and wild onions, and still had a supply of cornmeal for the grainy *pinole*.

Climbing the steep rock wall was just one more proof that Bootless Warrior and the others were stronger than Miguel, and completely at home in the desert or in the mountains. Miguel tried to ignore the fringe of hair that hindered his vision and the pain that coursed through his shoulders. Cautiously, he curled his bare toes into narrow slits in the rock. He slid one hand higher, groping for a thin ledge that might support his weight. His fingers hooked into a shallow indentation, but when he rested his weight against it, the rock crumbled and he began to slip.

Without a word, Stone Face nudged his shoulder against Miguel's rump. Steadied enough to continue, Miguel found another razor-thin crevice to support his fingers. Stone Face continued to climb, supporting Miguel from beneath. As Miguel stretched for one final pull, Line Leader reached down and yanked him over the top. Miguel's chest scraped across the jagged outcroppings, and he stifled a cry. The band already thought he was weak. He didn't need to prove it again.

Just below, Stone Face and the four remaining

warriors scaled the rock like sticky-toed lizards. Miguel had barely a moment for one last look at the dizzying height he had climbed before the group pushed on into the mountains. This time, Stone Face did not shove him into line. Instead, he pulled the headband from his head and offered it to Miguel. Was this a reward for climbing the cliff? Miguel would never have made it to the top without help. He took the faded cloth and tied it around his forehead, holding his hair away from his eyes. He was surprised that the wide strip of cloth served a useful purpose. He nodded his thanks, but Stone Face didn't react in any way.

Miguel struggled to keep his appointed place, fifth behind Line Leader, with five more Indé at his back. Like his shredded socks, the cotton bindings he had wrapped around his feet were in tatters and wouldn't last much longer.

In the past few days the band had climbed higher along the trail and the temperature had dropped steadily. Miguel shivered day and night without his shirt and was feverish with a cold that made his head feel as if it were stuffed with cotton. Line Leader glanced back as Miguel was seized with a fit of coughing that shook him to his bones.

Bootless Warrior trotted alongside and shoved the tip of his bow against Miguel's stomach. "Boy is soft," he said derisively. Miguel stiffened, determined to prove him wrong. He wiped at his dripping nose with the back of his hand and hurried to keep pace. He had to keep up to stay alive.

The men emerged into the sunlight, and Miguel welcomed its warmth. From the desert floor where his journey had begun, to the higher peaks of the mountains, the landscape had completely changed. Wildflowers sprouted between rocks, grappling for a foothold just as Miguel had while climbing the rock face. Creosote bushes and brittle bush burst with yellow spring blossoms that nodded and bobbed while bees flitted between them.

The silence around Miguel made him feel as if he were slowly disappearing. He longed to talk with someone just to feel that he was still Miguel. How different it would be to explore these mountains with his brothers and Papá. *I've never been so far from home*, he thought.

Jacob Franck's words echoed in his fuzzy head: *how good it is to hear the language of the Old Country.* Now Miguel understood the peddler's feelings. Even if his brothers called him *Miguelito*, he would welcome the sound. *How good it is . . .* He trudged forward in a daze. He had hours to walk on his cut feet before he could rest for the night.

Surely by now Papá knows I've been captured, he thought. *The commander at Fort Lowell must have sent out troops.* Miguel stealthily felt for the jackknife hidden in his pocket. If just a single warrior guarded him, he might have a chance to use it and make an escape. Or if his captors left him alone at night, he might be able to cut their bowstrings while they slept and slip away. Miguel was never tied up, but he was watched every moment.

At camp that evening, Miguel sat in a darkened spot apart from the others. He unwound the strips of shredded cloth from his feet as the warriors sat around a low fire. Their voices were soft, but for the first time Miguel detected a note of anger, taut as a bowstring ready to shoot. One by one, each warrior spoke, and his companions listened without interruption. At home, discussions around the dinner table often turned into arguments with his brothers. Sometimes they all bellowed at once, until no one could hear the opinions of the others. Among the Indé there had been no arguments—until tonight.

Bootless Warrior squatted close to the fire and

spoke in an angry growl. When he finished, Line Leader rose to his full height, settling the horse blanket around his shoulders like a prince's cape. He spoke in an even tone, holding each man in his gaze for a moment. His hands cut the air in a spreading motion, as if smoothing the ripples on a patch of windswept sand.

Stone Face spoke in turn, his voice insistent. He gestured toward Bootless Warrior. Miguel had an uneasy sense that they were arguing about him. He watched closely, trying to learn what he could from their gestures and their tone.

Suddenly, Bootless Warrior pulled an arrow from his quiver and stabbed it into the earth. "*Pindah-lickoyee*," he shouted, curling his upper lip into a sneer.

Miguel's body tensed as an uneasy silence settled over the group. He shrank into the shadows, but Line Leader stepped forward and pulled him into the circle, gripping his arm tightly. The warrior talked and pointed repeatedly at Miguel.

The campfire's flames licked at the dead cactus wood and cast a red glow across the faces that glared up at him. Miguel tried to stand tall, but he was seized with fear. What did it all mean?

Line Leader shouldered his bow and quiver and gave an order to the group in a voice so low it sounded like the growl of a dog about to attack. He kicked a spray of sand across the fire, and the rest of the band immediately gathered their belongings. Stone Face smothered the fire completely and scattered the hot ashes while another man swept the area with a pine branch, erasing every trace of their footprints.

Line Leader pointed Miguel back into his place, and they filed away from camp. The argument and the sudden return to the trail seemed a dangerous sign. *We've never traveled at night before.* Maybe the warriors had not been arguing about him. Perhaps they were simply disagreeing about whether or not to continue walking in the dark. *But why did Line Leader pull me in front of the group?* Miguel worried.

With a brief flutter of hope, he wondered if a search party had been sighted, forcing the men to keep moving. Was there a chance he might be rescued?

The group walked more slowly in the dark, but still traveled faster than Miguel wished. His feet were swollen and tender from the cuts he had received along the trail. He hoped the night air was too cold for rattlesnakes or tarantulas to venture out. He didn't want to tread on one of them in the dark.

Bootless Warrior stepped behind him, and Miguel felt the warrior's breath hot against his neck. This was the first time Stone Face hadn't been at his back, and Miguel felt a ripple of fear race up his spine. If Line Leader had overruled Bootless Warrior's argument at the campfire, the younger man might be angry. *But it wasn't my doing*, Miguel thought. Several members of the band seemed to side with Bootless Warrior, but clearly Line Leader had made the decision to move on.

Miguel longed for the sound of hoof beats. He hoped the cavalry had found his trail. *Jesus, Mary, and Joseph*, he prayed silently, *help me in my hour of need*.

Miguel raised his arm to make the sign of the cross when he was struck from behind without warning. He cried out as pain pierced his left shoulder, and he stumbled to the ground. Bootless Warrior stood above him holding a stout branch.

"*Pindah-lickoyee!*" the warrior shouted. In the weak moonlight, Miguel saw him lift the stick to strike again.

"No!" he yelled. Miguel raised his right arm to protect himself, but the stick crashed against his head. Searing pain coursed through his temple, and Miguel felt a warm trickle of blood seep under his headband and over his eye.

Stone Face jumped on Bootless Warrior, grappling for control of the stick. Miguel cowered at the edge of the trail as the two men fell to the ground in a fierce struggle.

A whipping sound cut the air as a dark shadow swooped overhead, and an owl's cry ripped eerily through the night like a shriek. *To-whoo! To-whoo!*

Stone Face and Bootless Warrior stopped fighting as if on command, and the rest of the band stood as still as statues. Miguel sensed the fear that ran through them like a finger of lightning that crackles the air before a storm.

He tried to reach for his knife, but his left arm dangled uselessly at his side. *I've got to escape,* he thought, struggling to rise. *This is my chance!* He pushed himself up with his right arm, and a sickening wave of dizziness washed over him. The warriors seemed to shimmer in the moonlight. Miguel swayed unsteadily, but no one made a move toward him.

The ghostly white face of an owl swept down as the men crouched on the path. Its eerie screech faded into the distance along with the sound of its beating wings. As if released from a spell, the warriors ran off in disarray.

Miguel steadied himself and stumbled back down the trail until he was alone. He teetered at the edge of a steep slope, considering how to climb down, when a threatening voice whispered from the darkness.

"*Pindah-lickoyee*," it breathed, the voice filled with contempt. Cold fear tightened Miguel's throat and rooted him to the path as Bootless Warrior stepped from behind a bush. He swung his club against Miguel's ribs, knocking him backward, over the edge of the steep path.

Miguel tumbled like a kicked stone, his body striking against jagged rocks, branches, and cactus spines. Unable to stop, he plunged over the last precipice, dropping senseless onto the desert floor below.

CHAPTER 8
The Scorpion's Sting

Scorching sun burned Miguel's bare chest, and his eyes fluttered open. He squinted against the strong light. Dark images of last night's scuffle flashed into his memory before he remembered where he was.

I'm alive, he thought. *I still have a chance to get home.* Miguel brushed away a host of swarming flies and felt sticky blood oozing beneath his headband. He gingerly touched a gash at his forehead.

In spite of his wound, he felt a rush of relief. *At least Bootless Warrior hasn't found me. Not yet.* The Indé traveled fast, and without Miguel to slow them down, they would move more swiftly. He tried to raise his left arm, but excruciating pain shot from his shoulder to his fingertips. His arm hung limply, broken or torn from its socket. With each breath, sharp stabs of pain radiated from his ribs.

Miguel tried to push himself up with his good arm, but the strain of moving overwhelmed him. He slumped to the ground. Slowly, Miguel rolled onto his stomach, cactus thorns pressing into his skin. *I've got to get out of the sun before it dries up every drop of moisture left in my body,* he told himself. *And I have to get out of sight.* If he didn't hide, he would be an easy target for Bootless Warrior's arrows.

Not far ahead, Miguel saw the lime-green bark of a paloverde tree at the base of the mountain. Its pale leaves sheltered a cluster of bushes. If only he could reach it, there would be some shade under its slender branches.

Using one arm, Miguel dragged himself across the gravelly sand and scrubby brush. The desert around him was so silent he could hear his heartbeat pulsing in his ears. After just a few minutes of effort, he had to rest. The tree hardly seemed any closer, but Miguel glanced back to gauge how far he had come. The impression of his body stood out in the sand like the flat trail of a giant snake. The Indé had wiped away every trace of their footprints as they traveled. Miguel's wide track would be easy to follow, but he couldn't retrace his path to erase it. He struggled forward another few inches.

After what seemed like hours, Miguel made one final push and curled up against the trunk of the low tree. His skin was raw from dragging himself across the sand, and his sunburned chest felt as if it had been singed over a flame. He closed his eyes in the cooling shade and drifted in and out of sleep.

When Miguel awakened fully, the sun was low and the air was rapidly growing cold. He couldn't get used to the extreme temperature changes that he had to endure each day. A fit of coughing racked his body, and he moaned with pain. He ran his dry tongue over his parched lips. *When was the last time I drank any water?*

Miguel sat up, wincing at the barbed cactus thorns that pierced his arms, chest, and back. He tried to grasp the tips of the thin spines, but they slipped through his fingers. Using his fingernails, he gripped them firmly and tugged. He managed to pull out a few thorns. The barbs left small ragged cuts, and Miguel rubbed the tender spots. It would be soothing to wash them in cool water, but he wasn't likely to find any now. He pictured the well in Tucson where the women filled *ollas* to the brim. Spilled water splashed at their feet while they laughed. *Dear God,* he vowed silently, *I'll never again take such a blessing for granted.*

A soft scratching sound broke the silence, and Miguel crouched closer to the tree. Peering from his hiding place, he spotted a streaked black-and-white roadrunner scratching at the pebbly sand and pecking at bugs. The bird's long tail feathers flicked, and the feathers on the crown of its head were as ruffled as hair tousled in the wind.

The scrawny desert chicken was more feathers than flesh, but Miguel thought that if he could kill it he could get moisture and nourishment from its meat. With the barest movement, he picked up a stone. Staring the bird into focus, he took careful aim and hurled the stone at its tawny head. His throw was wide of the mark. Miguel felt bitter disappointment as the startled fowl simply flapped out of range.

I couldn't have cooked it, anyway, he argued to himself. But he knew he would have eaten it raw, if necessary. Despite the time he spent with the band of warriors, Miguel hadn't gotten used to eating only once each day. His stomach rumbled. He might survive without food for a few days, but not without water. How had the Indé discovered so many water holes? He glanced at the rocks towering overhead. The last water hole where the warriors had dipped their gourds was high up on the trail.

The path he had traveled was both distant and dangerous. He couldn't climb with his injured arm, and even if he could, he risked being captured again. He had to find water, but how?

Miguel turned his face away from the setting sun. Purple shadows crept over the rocky crevices and fell in jagged patterns across the boulders. *How can I make my way across the desert?* He had heard of silver mines outside Tucson. Maybe he'd come across a mining camp. If he was lucky, he might find a wagon trail and meet a caravan of travelers. There was always a chance he would cross paths with a lone peddler like Jacob Franck who would take him home.

A surge of loneliness washed over him, and Miguel realized that the peddler's companionship would now be welcome. *I ran from him and the awful words he read, but what did I run to?*

Miguel's thoughts surged back to his life in Tucson. It seemed so far away. *When I helped with Mass, I thought God was calling me to serve Him and the church. Father Ignacio said that one day I would know the right choice in my heart.* After all that had happened, Miguel only felt emptiness. Perhaps God was testing his faith. Or worse, maybe He was telling Miguel that he had no place as a priest.

An image of the quiet interior of the dim church filled his head. He saw himself on his last Sunday at Mass, moving toward the Communion railing behind Father Ignacio. He couldn't get past the sense that he was shadowing the priest so he would one day serve Communion to his own parishioners.

The image persisted like a blurry dream. He could almost hear Father Ignacio ring the silver bells three times, calling the congregants to receive the wafer that represented the body of Christ. Miguel remembered his mother and brothers rising from their pew and coming forward. His mother's hair was covered by her lace *mantilla.* As the priest placed the thin, flat bread upon each worshipper's tongue, he intoned the Latin prayer that began, "*Corpus Domini nostril Jesu Christi . . .*" Miguel joined in a fervent *amen* at its conclusion.

Papá hung back that morning. As Miguel held the silver patina close to each person who received a wafer, he noticed Papá looking worried and distant, as if troubling thoughts had brought him far away. As soon as Miguel caught his eye, Papá hurried to the railing, kneeling before the altar.

Had Papá been wondering when he should tell Miguel about their Israelite ancestor? Until the night when the peddler read from the leather diary, Miguel had been secure in his beliefs. With just a few words read from a crumbling book, his life had changed completely. He no longer felt certain of anything—not his family, not his calling, not his very self.

Miguel tried to snap out of the vision that clouded his thoughts. He had to stop daydreaming and start walking. If he observed the desert around him more closely, he might find water. It had been days since he had run from the ranch. *By now, they've all given up any chance of finding me,* he realized. *It's up to me to get home. Only me.*

Shadows lengthened and Miguel pulled himself up, clinging to the tree for support. He spit out the dust that coated his throat and staggered forward. Cactus thorns pricked his back and arms with the slightest movement, but Miguel couldn't stay where he was.

He would keep the mountains on his right and continue traveling south, walking only at night when the desert was cool and darkness would hide him. Miguel reassured himself that the Indé weren't likely to venture onto a trail at night ever again. He was amazed that the strong warriors who roamed the desert like antelope and endured cold and hunger without complaint were so easily frightened by the screech of an owl.

How many days have I been walking? he wondered. He counted each day on his fingers, recalling the events of each one until the moment when he had been pushed off the ledge. Five days, he realized with a shock. *Tomorrow is my birthday. If I make it through one more night, I will be thirteen.*

A crescent moon lit the sky, and Miguel's eyes slowly adjusted. Stars flickered as if someone had tossed a handful of glittering mica into the air. Miguel picked out the brightest as the North Star and carefully kept it behind him.

Papá had often tried to teach Miguel to name the constellations, but the task had seemed boring and useless. Miguel had no interest in learning to recognize the shapes and patterns his father pointed out. *If only I'd known that I would need to find my way across the desert by their light, I would have listened*, he thought with regret.

He remembered the words Señor Franck had read from the diary. Aharon ben Avraham had used his skills as a mapmaker to chart a path across the desert. He must have been familiar with every constellation in the sky. Miguel had tried to deny his connection to the first Abrano. Now he wished the mapmaker could guide him home before it was too late.

A coyote howled in the distance, and a chorus of yips answered from another direction. Miguel glanced around, straining to see into the distance. With the arrival of night, the desert had come alive with sounds. Insects buzzed and chirped, and dry brush rustled around him. He didn't know what made the noises or whether they posed a danger. All he could do was push forward.

Suddenly there was a faint clatter of loose gravel from the mountain trail above. Miguel froze. Were the Indé tracking him? Or was a stealthy puma looking for an easy meal? Miguel felt so weak that he had no chance of outrunning anyone—animal or man. The coyotes let out a mournful chorus of howls. As long as he heard them in the mountains, Miguel guessed they were not hunting him. A mountain lion—or a bootless warrior—would stalk him silently.

A cascade of small stones and sand tumbled down the slope. Narrowing his eyes, Miguel thought he glimpsed a moving shape, barely a shadow. Someone, or something, was watching him.

He edged toward a large saguaro, its arms branching upward like a sentinel giving a salute. He might be able to shelter near its thick trunk and disappear from view. He stepped closer to its thorny protection when an excruciating sting blazed through his bare foot. He let out a muffled cry as fiery heat spread rapidly up his leg. He barely glimpsed a small scurrying creature flicking its curling tail over its back before it darted into a hole in the sand.

Scorpion! He had to stop the poison from coursing through his entire body. His foot swelled as quickly as a bubble rising in hot fat. Miguel fumbled to tie his headband tightly around his ankle, hoping to stop the poison's flow. Then he remembered the pocketknife and pulled it out, struggling to open the blade. Gripping the knife tightly, he slashed his foot where the scorpion had stung. He had to drain the venom before it spread. A hot dizziness swept over him, and Miguel dropped to his knees.

CHAPTER 9
Son of Rain Stalker

Miguel dreamed he was running across the desert, chased by Indé shooting cactus spines into his bare back. As each prickly needle pierced his skin, he flinched in pain. Miguel darted left and right, but couldn't escape their attack. He panted with exhaustion, wondering how much longer he could keep running.

Caught between wakefulness and sleep, Miguel wondered if the pain was part of his dream—or if it was real. His eyes fluttered open, and with a rising fear, he saw two deep black eyes staring at him. The warriors had found him! This time, Miguel wouldn't let them take him without a fight.

Seeing his open knife on the sand, he seized it and stabbed in the direction of his enemy. The glinting blade cut the air harmlessly, and the mere effort of waving it sapped Miguel's last reservoir of strength.

Without showing the slightest fear, the person looming above him took the knife, folded it with a snap, and placed it back in Miguel's hand. The handle felt cool against his sweaty palm.

Miguel heard a voice so soft that he wondered if he were still dreaming, "I am not your enemy," the voice said. "I am Tohono O'odham friend."

Miguel tried to understand where he was. Instead of the saguaro where he had stopped last night, he was in the shade of the mountain under a rocky outcropping. He reached up and felt a tattered cloth tied just above his eye. A poultice of soft leaves soothed the knife wound, and his foot was tightly bound with a blue cloth bandage.

Another strip of my clothes gone, he thought, recognizing pieces of cloth from his pants legs. An unfamiliar red neckerchief cradled his limp arm in a tight sling.

The young man eased Miguel against the rock and held a gourd of water to his mouth. Miguel gulped in desperate swallows. A faint bitter taste lingered, but as Miguel drank he felt his tight chest loosening.

"More water," he begged.

"Drink slow," his companion advised, holding the gourd back for a moment. When Miguel had drained the last drop of water, he studied the young man. His hair was cropped short, a gray muslin shirt was tied around his waist, and he wore baggy cotton pants tied at the waist with rope. Sandals woven from braided grass protected his feet. As far as Miguel could see, he carried no weapon. He couldn't be Indé. But what tribe was called Tohono O'odham?

"Can you eat?" the Indian asked. He held out a stick of roasted meat, and Miguel recognized the smell of cooked rabbit. He savored the first bite, letting the fatty richness slide into his empty stomach.

Miguel saw no fire, but noticed a ring of stones piled nearby. He could feel heat radiating from them, yet there was no flame. How could anyone cook a rabbit without a fire?

"I am Rushing Cloud, son of Rain Stalker, son of I'itoi, the Creator," said the young man. "And you?"

Miguel tensed. Father Ignacio would explain about God to such a heathen, but Miguel kept silent. If Rushing Cloud stayed with him, Miguel would find the right time to show him the truth.

"What are you called?" the young man persisted.

Miguel hesitated. Who was he now? He was the son of his father, Mateo Abrano. Was he also ben Avraham? *That isn't part of me*, he determined. *I won't let it be.*

He sucked in his breath. "I am Miguel," he said simply. He chewed another mouthful of meat and soon finished every morsel on the stick. He lay back down and realized with relief that no cactus thorns bit into his back.

"Did you pull out all those spines?" Miguel asked.

His companion nodded. "I have watched you in the desert," he explained. "At first, I was afraid— afraid you are a white enemy searching for me. Then I see you are just a boy wandering. You eat nothing. You drink nothing. I think, *this boy will die soon.*"

A flare of anger rose in Miguel's chest. Even this stranger thought of him as a boy and not a man. Yet today he was thirteen, and as weak as he was, he was still alive. Still, Miguel couldn't deny that in spite of what he had endured along the trail, he hadn't become a man just because he had turned one year older.

Miguel was grateful for Rushing Cloud's help, but why had he waited so long?

"You thought I would die, but you just left me alone?" Miguel demanded. "I stepped on a scorpion trying to hide because I thought you were a warrior stalking me, or a mountain lion."

"Enemies and mountain lions do not watch," said Rushing Cloud evenly. "They kill." Now Rushing Cloud asked his own questions. "Why are you in the desert with no white companions? Were you with a wagon train that was attacked?"

"I was alone from the beginning," Miguel said. Rushing Cloud waited expectantly for more.

Miguel couldn't admit that he had run away from home without a plan. Surely he would seem worse than a child—he'd look like a fool. Rushing Cloud would never understand what Miguel had learned that night at the ranch. Now he was no longer certain what he had been running from. Was it the revelation about his family, or the shame of his tears?

"I was riding, and I—I got lost," he stammered. "I camped for the night in a stand of cottonwoods. I thought I'd find my way home in the morning, but I was captured by a band of warriors who stole my horse and my boots. At first, I thought they were Apache, but they got angry when I said that. They called themselves Indé."

"You make them angry," Rushing Cloud explained. "*Apachu* is what others call them. It means 'enemy.' They think they are *Indé*, The People." He made a sound that was half sneer and half horselaugh. "As if they are the First People."

Miguel shivered. *So, they were Apache*, he thought.

"*Apachu* raid in small bands. They hide in the desert at night. They must have been stalking travelers to steal horses and food. Then you come along and they decide to keep you instead. No fighting, no more searching, and they return to camp with a valuable catch. They think you can become a warrior like them. If not, you will work for the women in the camp—carry wood and water, do woman's work."

So that would have been my life, Miguel realized. If he had stayed "soft," as Bootless Warrior called him, he would have become a slave in the Apache camp. If not, he would have trained to be like them, heading out on his own raids.

Rushing Cloud frowned. "How you got away?"

Every part of Miguel was shutting down with exhaustion. He hadn't spoken so many words in nearly a week. His face flushed with fever, yet a wave of chills washed over him. He curled up on the ground. In a hoarse whisper he asked, "Why did you help me?"

"It is what a man must do," Rushing Cloud said. He draped his shirt over Miguel's shoulders, covering him with comforting warmth. "Sleep now," he said, "for tonight we must walk far." As Miguel drifted into sleep, he thought he heard Rushing Cloud murmur, "Scorpion has chosen you."

* * *

Miguel awoke as dusk settled. His fever had cooled as quickly as the desert air. He sat up against the rock wall, looking for his companion. Faint music filtered toward him. Miguel looked a short distance away and saw Rushing Cloud sitting cross-legged under the open sky, his head hanging down against his chest. He sang a soft melody, filled with repeated sounds. His voice was high, each note pure and clear.

Seeming to sense that Miguel was watching him, Rushing Cloud stopped chanting and loped back to the shelter. In a barely audible voice he said, "The night comes and we must walk." He helped Miguel to his feet.

"What were you singing?" Miguel asked. He felt stronger, although he couldn't put any pressure on his injured foot.

"I am singing of our journey, of the way it will be. I tell I'itoi, the Creator, how he must help us. In the coolness of the night, in the shadow of the mountain, we will walk. Long will be walk, never tiring, never thirsting, like stars walking across the sky."

Miguel was mesmerized by the sound of Rushing Cloud's gentle voice. Yet it wasn't a song, he realized. It was a prayer. Could a heathen's words be called that? Father Ignacio was certain that only the prayers of the faithful were heard and answered. Still, Miguel knew that the voices of the natives had chanted to their gods long before the church began. The prayers of his Abrano ancestors had surely risen to God, as well.

Miguel lifted his eyes to the brightening moon. The last time he had asked God's help was on the trail. He had prayed to be rescued. Would his prayers and Rushing Cloud's both be answered? Which god was listening?

Miguel handed back the shirt, but Rushing Cloud merely tied it around his waist. He scattered the cold stones that had smoldered earlier and brushed all traces of their tracks from the sand. "We must leave no footsteps for others to follow."

Miguel limped from the shelter, Rushing Cloud keeping a slow pace beside him. He pointed to Miguel's foot. "Scorpion is your guardian now," he said. "He will give you power."

"That's pretty generous," Miguel said. "Being stung certainly didn't make me feel powerful."

"It is your own knife that has hurt you the most," Rushing Cloud countered. "Scorpion is sending you a sharp message. He says you have power to survive in the desert with little food or water, as he does. He will help you."

Miguel looked up at the skies again, seeing a flurry of stars. They seemed close enough to touch.

Rushing Cloud followed his gaze. "Some say scorpion watches the stars to guide his path across the desert," he said. "If you watched them to begin your journey home, then perhaps scorpion has already guided you."

"I only know one star," Miguel mumbled, ashamed of his own ignorance. "I guess I'm not as smart as a scorpion." He pointed to the brightest star in the heavens. "My father told me that one is always to the north. I know the Indé brought me north into the mountains, as the star was always ahead. I'm pretty sure I have to travel south to get back to my family's ranch, so I've been trying to keep that North Star at my back." He thought for a moment. "How do you know scorpions can read the position of the stars?"

"The elders tell it," Rushing Cloud said.

Miguel felt a touch of annoyance. Rushing Cloud seemed so sure of everything, as if he had no doubts in his mind. Miguel suddenly realized that he was no different. Only a week ago, he had been convinced he knew everything he needed. When Papá had tried to teach him about the positions of the stars, Miguel was sure it was useless to learn. When Papá had talked about the family's history, Miguel had never suspected that Papá had not revealed what he truly had needed to know. What could he believe in now?

Rushing Cloud was quiet, striding through the darkness as if he were strolling down the main street in Tucson. Miguel didn't know why, but he felt confident that Rushing Cloud would guide him home. Only a week ago, he never would have imagined that an Indian could be trusted at all.

As the night stretched on, Miguel's hobbling progress became more and more difficult. His bandaged foot began to bleed, and he couldn't put any weight on it. He bent his knee and placed the pressure on his heel. Soon his good leg cramped from the extra weight and the unnatural position as he limped along. Rushing Cloud got farther and farther ahead until Miguel had difficulty keeping him in sight.

"Wait," he called softly. "I've got to rest."

Rushing Cloud paused until Miguel caught up. "I will carry you," he offered, bending down. Miguel barely hesitated before he climbed onto Rushing Cloud's back, bracing his good arm across his companion's chest while he held Miguel's legs. Rushing Cloud kept a swift pace. "We must walk until the sun warms the air," he said. "First light is already upon us." Miguel scanned the horizon, but everything looked black.

Rushing Cloud began chanting softly. Miguel didn't understand the words, but they began to sound familiar as the young man repeated them over and over in the same tone. He wondered if it was the same song Rushing Cloud had explained earlier. Lulled by the sound and the steady rhythm of his companion's steps, he dozed against Rushing Cloud's sturdy back.

When Miguel next looked up, the sun was sending its first rays of rosy light over the desert. "I'll try to walk again," he offered and eased himself down.

Rushing Cloud pointed to an outcropping of rocks in the distance. The yellow blossoms of a few early-blooming creosote bushes stood out like tiny candles in the shadows.

"There we will build a shelter. It will be cool against the rocks, and we will find water." He trotted ahead.

How could Rushing Cloud be so certain that there would be water? It didn't seem as if he had been here before. Miguel gimped along toward the shadowy boulders. Rushing Cloud was already gathering sticks and small branches and setting them across two jagged rocks that jutted out overhead. Using his right hand, Miguel began collecting dry brush to add to the shelter. Low barrel cacti crowned with waxy yellow flowers and flat prickly pear cacti clustered near scattered clumps of thick grasses. The leaves of a gnarled mesquite tree filtered shadows across the sandy soil.

"With the rocks at our backs," Rushing Cloud explained, "no one can sneak up behind us. The brush will hide us from our enemies and from the heat of the sun." Miguel saw that the shelter faced east. The early morning sun would not be as hot, and by afternoon when its rays were most oppressive, the sun would drop behind the rocks, leaving them in shade. Rushing Cloud seemed to know all this by instinct.

Miguel thought about the band of Apache. "I don't think the warriors are tracking me or they would have caught up long before now," he said. "Maybe they stayed away because you're with me. Although, if they wanted new warriors, you're definitely the better choice." Like the Indé, Rushing Cloud was swift and at ease in the desert. Like them, he didn't seem to feel the extremes of heat or cold. Miguel thought the natives were truly part of the desert, and it was part of them.

When the shelter was completed, Rushing Cloud stepped among the grasses. He found a flat stone and began to scrape at the sandy ground between the boulders.

"Where is the iron point?" he asked, and Miguel handed him the pocketknife. Without hesitation,

Rushing Cloud used the blade to dig deeper. Miguel saw that the sand looked darker. As his companion widened the hole, water seeped in. "Drink," Rushing Cloud said. They cupped their hands, grateful for the few drops of water that had been hidden just beneath the surface.

"How did you know there was water here?" Miguel asked.

"The elders tell that green grass always stands with its feet wet," Rushing Cloud answered.

Miguel couldn't believe that someone his own age knew so much about living in the desert. He was ashamed of his own weakness. Not so long ago, he had argued with his family and bragged about his skills. He had longed for the chance to prove his independence, but he had failed. If Rushing Cloud hadn't helped him, his birthday might have been his last day.

The two companions pushed closer together in the cramped shelter. Looking across the brightening desert, Miguel saw another roadrunner poised on a rock. Its feathery crest spiked up and then flattened against its head. Miguel touched Rushing Cloud's arm to show him the bird, but the young man was already studying it.

Miguel reached for a loose stone. The bird was a swift runner, but it could barely fly. *This time, my aim will be better*, he thought. *I will show Rushing Cloud that I can take care of myself.*

As he raised his hand, Rushing Cloud held Miguel's arm down. In a barely audible voice, he murmured, "Watch."

CHAPTER 10
Snake Killer

The tawny cock stood as still as a fence post. Miguel also froze, afraid the slightest movement would scare it off. The bird's feathers mixed mottled shades of brown and black with streaks of white, providing camouflage.

A stealthy motion in the sand drew Miguel's attention. Just in front of the bird, a thick-bodied rattlesnake slithered toward their shelter. Yellow scales tinged the diamond pattern along its back, and its tongue darted in and out, testing the air for the scent of prey. Miguel had always been told a rattler wouldn't attack if you didn't move. It was one piece of advice he had followed. The skin on his back prickled, and he wondered if he could remain as calm and still as Rushing Cloud.

The snake slid closer, its movements both contorted and graceful. Miguel silently prayed the snake would change direction. Just as it entered a bright patch of sunlight, the roadrunner flapped down. Its long, sharp beak was poised for attack.

The snake opened its jaws wide, baring its fangs. Its tail rattles vibrated an ominous warning, but the bird kept up its sniping. Aiming for a spot just behind the snake's head, it landed a fearless peck. The snake coiled and sprang at the bird, which flapped out of range and then charged again. Attacking and retreating, the two adversaries seemed determined to fight to the death.

"Rattlesnakes cannot live long under the sun," Rushing Cloud whispered. "It is a creature of night." Miguel watched the battle with awe. The roadrunner toyed with the snake, luring it farther into the blazing sun, attacking just often enough to keep it from escaping under the rocks. The rattler became sluggish, either tiring from the fight or suffering from the rising heat.

The bird's attacks grew bolder and more deadly, striking deep into the rattler's flesh. When the snake failed to respond to one ferocious peck, the bird boldly caught the large reptile in its beak and dashed it against a rock. The snake struggled, but its wounds were too severe.

Miguel was riveted to the final moments of the duel. The bird made one last attack, tearing a deep wound at the back of the reptile's head. The rattler gave a convulsive shake and lay still in the sun. As the roadrunner dove in to devour its kill, Rushing Cloud sprang from the shelter waving his arms up and down. The victorious bird cast its glassy orange-rimmed eyes on its prey and then looked with alarm at the intruder. It raced off across the sand, its tail straight and its beak thrust forward like the point of an arrow.

Rushing Cloud grabbed the limp snake by the tail and held it up like a trophy. It was longer than he was tall. A small smile curled at the corner of his mouth. "Dinner," he said.

Miguel stepped closer. "You're going to eat it?" he asked.

"No," Rushing Cloud said. "You are."

Miguel knew that the ranch hands occasionally ate a rattlesnake they had killed. The thought of eating a poisonous reptile that moments before had been slithering toward him seemed only slightly less appetizing than eating Doc Meyer's horse. At least he hadn't been friends with the snake.

Miguel looked down at his feet. All around him, the sand was marked with curious X-shaped prints. He couldn't guess what they were. Rushing Cloud noticed Miguel's puzzled look.

"We call this snake-killer *todai*," Rushing Cloud said. "*Todai* is both brave and clever." He turned over various stones, testing their sharpness and tossing them aside. "With two toes pointed forward and two backward, who can follow his trail?" Miguel wouldn't have known which way the bird had run if he had been tracking it. "It is never wise to let your enemies know which way you have gone," Rushing Cloud added. Finally, he chose a long narrow stone with a rough edge and laid the dead snake in the shade.

Using his water gourd as a shovel, Rushing Cloud began digging a shallow, circular pit. Miguel helped scoop away the dirt as his companion loosened it. Then Rushing Cloud gathered several small rocks and used them to line the bottom of the hole. Next, he carefully arranged a pile of dried sticks topped with dry grass. Patiently, he struck a flint from his pocket against a rough stone until a spark flew onto the tinder and it began to smoke.

Rushing Cloud leaned into the smoking brush and blew steady streams of air until flames flickered and grew.

Miguel scoured the area, gathering pieces of cactus wood and withered twigs. The fire burned until there was neither flame nor smoke, but simply shimmering air radiating from the hot stones. Now he understood how Rushing Cloud had cooked the rabbit last night. The rocks held the heat long after the wood had burned to ashes. Without smoke or flame, no one would notice their hiding place.

Rushing Cloud bent over the snake's carcass and began to gut it. Miguel withdrew his pocketknife and opened the blade. He handed it to his companion, who tested it cautiously against his finger.

"Sharp," he grunted approvingly. "Now it is our Snake Skinner." Rushing Cloud sliced open the snake and removed the innards. With one strong cut, he chopped off the snake's venomous head and then severed the rattles from its tail. He cut the carcass into small sections and dropped them into the pit. Dripping juices hissed against the hot stones.

The boys crouched in the shade, watching the meat cook. Rushing Cloud played with the rattles, shaking them until they clattered their familiar warning. He handed them to Miguel. "If ever you are hiding and fear you will be discovered, use these to scare your enemy away."

Miguel tested the bony rattles until he could vibrate them easily. "You might need them—and you earned them," he said, offering them back.

Rushing Cloud turned the pieces of meat with a stick. "I already know many tricks, and the rattles may give you some of the snake's power." Rushing Cloud spoke so often of gaining power from animals. Miguel didn't understand, but he pushed the bony tail into his pocket.

Gingerly, Miguel tested his left arm. He still couldn't move it without searing pain. If anything, it felt worse than it had the first day he had been injured. The sling kept it from pulling against his shoulder socket, but he worried that something was terribly wrong since it hadn't begun to mend.

The gash on his foot was healing. It seemed Rushing Cloud had been right that the greatest injury had been the cut Miguel had made himself. He massaged the tender wound lightly. What he had done might seem foolish, but Miguel had been convinced that there was no choice. He couldn't know for certain what had bitten him in the dark. It might have been a more poisonous scorpion whose venom would have killed him in a matter of hours if he hadn't drained the poison before it spread.

Running away from home now seemed foolish, as well. Miguel was ashamed that just as he had slashed his foot without thinking of the consequences, he had run from the ranch without thinking of where he would go or what he would do. To think that he had been so heedless as to leave without even taking his hat!

Why didn't I realize I could get lost, or think about how frightened Mamá and Papá would be? Miguel had been faced with a choice, and he had made a childish one.

The waxy flowers on the creosote bush glowed in the sun's blazing light. Bees flitted from one blossom to another gathering pollen and making a droning buzz. As soon as they held their fill of pollen, they flew home. Miguel felt as if he had been away from his home for months instead of days.

"Why would the Apache take me so far?" he asked.

"They circle around, go high and then low. This makes it hard for anyone to find their camp—even you."

"They argued over what to do with me, I think," Miguel mused.

"Maybe some felt you would not become a strong warrior," Rushing Cloud said.

"I know I wasn't much of a prize," Miguel agreed. "I could barely keep up with them on the trail. I think some of them wanted to kill me. The last night I was with the band, a warrior hit me from behind. That's how my shoulder got hurt. I think he was going to finish me off, but an owl swooped across the path and they all ran."

A shadow of fear darkened Rushing Cloud's eyes. "An owl?" he repeated. "Owl is a messenger from the Spirit World, maybe the spirit of a dead person. Perhaps an ancestor came to help you. Owl warns them to beware." He was quiet for a moment and then murmured almost to himself, "So that is how you got away."

"I couldn't believe they were afraid of a bird when they seemed so brave about other things. They never complained about being cold or hungry or thirsty. They weren't afraid of being discovered by the cavalry. When they scattered, I ran too. I didn't think they saw me, but the warrior who had attacked me sneaked up and hit me again. I fell over the edge of the trail." Miguel's memory became clearer. "He said something other warriors had said that night, and his voice was angry. I don't remember the words exactly, but it sounded something like pin-da-lickee." Miguel's voice trailed off.

Rushing Cloud looked away. "*Pinduh lickoyee,*" he said in a soft voice. "White-eyed enemy."

CHAPTER 11
Trust the Inside

To the Apache, I am the enemy, Miguel mused. *To everyone else, they are the enemy.* The Apache had always claimed that the Abranos' horse ranch was on tribal land, even though the family had lived there for hundreds of years. It wasn't just the Abrano land the Apache wanted. They believed all white settlers were in their territory, and they wouldn't give up trying to remove them. Papá always said he would fight to his last breath if his land were threatened. Miguel realized now that the Apache felt the same.

Miguel thought again of the old diary. *What happened to the land Aharon ben Avraham left behind in Spain? If the church seized it, does that make the church my enemy?* Miguel rubbed his throbbing forehead.

What makes people enemies? he wondered. *Rushing Cloud was afraid that I was his enemy when he first noticed me, and I felt the same about him. But we have learned to trust each other. We call each other friend.*

Rushing Cloud scouted the area and picked up three dried-out cactus ribs. "Will you share Snake Skinner again?" he asked. Miguel pulled the knife from his pocket. Rushing Cloud used the blade to sharpen one end of each stick. With two of the sticks in hand, he walked to a prickly pear cactus. Holding the sticks like tongs, he gripped a spiny pad, sliced it off, and dropped it onto the sand. He repeated this a few more times.

"What are you doing?" Miguel asked.

"This is my dinner," his friend replied. Miguel watched as Rushing Cloud rubbed the cactus pads roughly over the pebbly sand. Most of the spines fell away, and the rest he pried out with the knife blade. As he worked, Rushing Cloud asked, "Has your family sent out soldiers to search for you?"

"At first, I was sure the cavalry would come," Miguel said. "Every day I listened for the sounds of hoof beats, hoping they had found my trail. I even wondered if their search was what made the Apache band decide to travel after dark the last night I was with them. Maybe they had seen soldiers and decided to move faster." He shook his head. "But I don't see how anyone could have tracked me. The band followed hidden trails into the mountains, and we even climbed up the face of a small cliff. No horse could follow us."

"And Apachu always leave false trails," Rushing Cloud said as he dropped the smooth cactus pads onto the hot stones in the fire pit. He sat down and pointed to Miguel's feet. "They take your boots, no?"

"Yes," Miguel answered. "One warrior put on my boots and walked off in a different direction than the rest of us. But when we arrived at a campsite that evening, he was already there—and my boots were gone."

"Apachu think of everything to hide," Rushing Cloud said with a hint of admiration for his enemy's skill. "What about your horse?"

Miguel tried to close his mind to what had happened to Zuzi. He answered tersely. "Another warrior took it."

"Yes," Rushing Cloud said, nodding knowingly. "Horse leaves tracks in one direction and boots make tracks another way. Then Apachu wipe out all other footprints. When soldiers find cottonwoods where you stayed, they look all around. They think horse ran off and you walked the wrong way. They never guess true direction the warriors take you. By the time they maybe figure it out, you are far away in enemy camp." Rushing Cloud's face lit up with amusement, as if he suddenly remembered a joke. "Sometimes, Apachu copy the tracks of our friend, Snake-Killer. They walk with moccasins on backwards. Looks like the warrior ended up where he started and then disappeared!" He paused and admitted, "I do that myself sometimes—like when I ran away."

Miguel was startled. "You ran away from home?"

Rushing Cloud looked puzzled. "No, I am running to my home. Why would I want to leave my family?" He jabbed the roasting cactus with a stick and turned it to char the other side.

Miguel swallowed hard. "What if—if your family wasn't who you thought they were? What if suddenly nothing was the same?"

Rushing Cloud shook his head. "People do not change. Maybe the outside looks a little different, but we trust what is inside."

Miguel's entire body felt heavy, as if he carried a weight he could not bear. He had lost trust in his own family. Each of them had known the story of Aharon ben Avraham, yet they had deliberately hidden it from him. Once again, they thought of him as a child, not a young man. Perhaps he had proven that they were right. Now he didn't know if he could even trust himself. He wasn't sure whether what was inside him was still the same. Miguel couldn't ask Rushing Cloud where he had run from, or he would have to admit what he had done.

"Dinner," Rushing Cloud said. He speared a shriveled piece of snake meat and handed it to Miguel.

Miguel pulled off the burnt papery skin and tentatively nibbled at the meat. He wiped the juices from his mouth with the back of his hand. "What about you?" he asked. "Aren't you going to eat some?"

Rushing Cloud skewered a cactus pad and waved it in the air to cool off. Carefully, he took a bite. "My people do not eat rattlesnake," he said. "The . . ."

". . . elders tell it," Miguel chimed in, finishing the sentence.

Rushing Cloud smiled. "You are learning," he said.

Miguel's stomach rumbled its hunger. He tried to forget what he was eating, and now took a large bite. Instead of sinking into thick meat, Miguel's teeth crunched against bones. The snake was a mass of sturdy ribs, as if the meat were hidden in a ring of toothpicks.

Now his companion couldn't hold back a laugh. "You are so hungry you eat bones?"

"I didn't even know snakes had bones," Miguel muttered sheepishly.

Rushing Cloud shook his head in disbelief. "I never eat this creature, but still I know it has bones."

Miguel took another bite, gnawing carefully at the stringy meat and pulling it away from the ribs where it held fast. The snake meat was tough, with a slightly bitter aftertaste. But the more Miguel ate, the more he grew accustomed to it. He stopped thinking of it as cooked rattlesnake and simply appreciated it as food. Before long, Miguel was cracking bones with his teeth to pull out every last shred of meat. When he finished the last piece, he wiped his hands on his pants.

Rushing Cloud collected the discarded pieces— bones, skin, head, and innards—and tossed them onto the still smoldering stones. He covered the pit with sand and wiped away traces of their meal with his feet.

"We need more water," Miguel said. "Let's go back to the hole you dug."

"Not safe," Rushing Cloud said. "We must stay out of sight." He sliced two more prickly pear pads from a different plant, pried out the spines, and made a cut across the top of each. He handed over one pad, and Miguel saw liquid dripping out. He licked at the moisture, then sucked the cut edge.

"It is not like water from the *olla*," Rushing Cloud noted, "but it will keep us."

"How do you know about getting water from a cactus?" Miguel asked.

Rushing Cloud responded with his own question. "How do you live in the desert and not know these things? Do you not see the rabbits and *javelinas* that chew cactus to get moisture? Do you not see anything around you?"

Miguel felt his face flush with embarrassment. It seemed that until now he hadn't looked at anything in his life with open eyes. He understood that it was time to think with his mind open, as well as his eyes.

The rattlesnake meat and the cactus juice satisfied his hunger and his thirst. Just a week ago, Miguel would never have been content with just one small meal each day or been able to survive in the desert with so little water. Perhaps he had become more like the scorpion. Maybe gaining power from another only meant that you learned new ways.

Rushing Cloud settled down in the shelter, folding his shirt for a pillow. Miguel stretched out beside him. "You never told me why you're traveling alone," said Miguel, hoping he wouldn't have to confess his own reason for becoming lost. Rushing Cloud lay on his back, staring up at the brush he had piled overhead.

For a long moment he was silent. Miguel wondered if his companion was hiding something, just as Miguel was. Then, in a challenging voice, Rushing Cloud said, "I ran away from the mission school." When Miguel offered no protest, Rushing Cloud began to share more.

"Many sleeps past," he said, "when the planting season was upon us, a white man with hair upon his face came to our *rancheria* driving a wagon. I see my cousins and other children from our village are already in the wagon. My father was away tending our fields, and my mother and sisters were under the ramada. If only I had gone to help my father that day, I might be there still." He paused, as if regretting what might have been. "This man tells my mother that all Indian children must go to a place where they will learn the new ways of white men. He said nothing about being forced to pray to their god."

Miguel swallowed the words that nearly leapt from his mouth. *That is my God*, he thought. *The only God.* Should he try to lead Rushing Cloud to the faith now? Clearly the missionaries had already tried to do that. And now Miguel was uncertain of what he had once believed was his calling.

"My mother tried to shield me from the hairy face man. With gestures, she tries to explain I am her only son—I am needed to work in the fields so we will have enough to eat. But the white man holds a paper my mother cannot read and tells her it is written that if she does not send me to this school, the white chiefs will lock my father in their iron cage. With tears flowing from her eyes, my mother scoops beans into a covered basket for the journey and fills an *olla* of water. As the man takes me to the wagon, my grandmother pulls me to her and whispers one last piece of wisdom for me to carry away. I did not forget her words."

Miguel sensed his friend's sadness and tried not to interrupt for fear that Rushing Cloud would stop speaking. "We traveled a long trail, through other villages where more children are taken and other wagons come to carry them. At each *rancheria*, the women give us dried cornmeal and fresh water. Soon everything I know is left behind. I never see my family again." Miguel guessed that the cornmeal was to make the same pasty *pinole* he had eaten along the trail. It was a poor meal—just enough to keep you alive.

"After four sleeps, we come to a white man's village, with wide trails leading to mud buildings. Women wearing strange clothes take all the girls away, and the boys are brought to a ramada. Some of the boys try to go after their sisters, but they are held back. Under the shade of the ramada, a man with an iron tool cuts off all our hair. If any boy fights against him, he is held down like a sheep losing its coat. Finally, we wash at wooden bowls and our clothes are taken away. The white men make us squeeze our feet into pinching boots. They show us how to make a button crawl into a hole in a cloth shirt. Everything is so tight against my skin that I feel that I cannot breathe."

Rushing Cloud sighed. "Never before did any Tohono O'odham boy cut his hair. We are ashamed to look upon each other." Then his voice rose in anger. "What had we done to make these people cut off our hair?" The question echoed off the rocks.

Rushing Cloud's short hair was the first thing Miguel had noticed, and it had reassured him that Rushing Cloud wasn't an Apache warrior. Miguel's own hair was long, and now it was dirty and matted. He even wore a headband like his captors, but that didn't make him an Apache.

Rushing Cloud hadn't chosen to cut his hair. He would have been the same even if his hair had reached his shoulders. Still, Miguel knew he would have been more afraid. Rushing Cloud kept talking as if a dam had opened, unleashing a stream of thoughts.

"Soon we are taken to a room where we must sit on long benches with our hands folded upon a board of wood. This they call a table, but we have never seen such a thing before. At the *rancheria*, we eat sitting on blankets spread on the soft sand and sleep on straw mats. At the school, bad-smelling food is put in front of us and the women make motions with their hands, telling us to eat. We try, but we cannot swallow such strange things. Day after day this is the only food they give us. Finally, we must eat or starve. The mission women become red in their faces if we do not eat everything placed before us. They whip us with sticks. But this food makes us sick, and we must run often to the wooden shed."

Miguel could never forget the rank smell of cooked horsemeat and the way his stomach had churned when he tried to eat it. Yet the Apache ate the meat with relish and laughed at his revulsion. He didn't think he would have grown to like horsemeat if he had lived with the Apache forever. Miguel could never erase the memory of seeing Doc Meyer's dead horse beyond the campfire.

Rushing Cloud spoke fiercely, his voice rising. "Some Pima boys are at the mission school too. Tohono O'odham are no friends of Pima. They laugh and call us *Papago*—Bean Eaters! Of course, we must fight for our honor." He pounded his fist against his chest. "We are Tohono O'odham, we tell them, People of the Desert!"

Miguel had always heard the Indians in Tucson called Papago. The women who came into town selling *ollas* and baskets, and the men who sometimes worked at the ranch, were all called Papago. It was the only term Miguel had ever known. Had he and his family been insulting these people without realizing it?

Miguel coughed. "Why didn't you and your cousins run away?" he asked.

"We are forbidden to speak our own tongue at the mission school, so we cannot make a plan together," said Rushing Cloud. His voice began to sound drowsy, but he kept talking. Miguel's eyelids drooped.

"At first, we do not understand English words, so how can we know that our own talk is not allowed?" he asked bitterly. "Whenever we spoke in our words, we were beaten and sometimes locked into a hot wooden box. There we sit and try to think of what we have done that is so terrible. Slowly, slowly, we learn the strange new talk. When we first come to the mission school it is the time of planting, when the earth is black with rain. By the time the corn stands tall our mouths only make the white man's sounds. Our own words begin to disappear like water hiding under the sand."

"You must trust the inside," Miguel said, using Rushing Cloud's own advice. "Your language is always in you."

Rushing Cloud turned his head toward Miguel, his eyes downcast. "We can accept the gods of the mission church, but we must not lose our own. Our sacred stories must be told every year, in the same words, always. It keeps our life in order. It makes the rain come and the fields to sprout. What will happen to my people if they forget their own tongue?"

Miguel thought of his ancestor's code. Maybe hearing Aharon Ben Avraham tell his story would keep his family's life in order too. Miguel realized that he had to at least listen.

CHAPTER 12
Back to the Blanket

When Miguel had started school in Tucson for the first time, all the students were required to speak English. He learned quickly, but still spoke Spanish with his friends, and at home. No one tried to make him forget his first language.

The Abranos' ranch had been part of Mexico until a huge swath of land was sold to the United States years before Miguel was born. It meant nothing to him until Papá explained that their family had suddenly become Americans with just the stroke of a pen. Inside, as Rushing Cloud would say, the family was still Mexican and they still spoke Spanish. No government could erase that. But they were American, as well.

Miguel shared Rushing Cloud's outrage that the missionaries had forbidden the native children from speaking their own languages. They could have taught them English and still let them use their own words outside the classroom.

A vision of his ancestor's tattered leather book flashed into Miguel's mind. If the Hebrew words were forgotten, who would be able to read the book again? Perhaps if you learned a new language—or a new religion—you could use one and still not throw away the other. Was that what his ancestor had done? What about Papá and Mamá?

Jacob Franck became the messenger carrying his ancestor's words. He relayed a story Papá cherished, and now Miguel felt ashamed of his lack of understanding. His angry words must have hurt Papá terribly. He tried to shake the image.

Miguel wondered if Rushing Cloud would someday tell his children and his grandchildren about the mission school. What had happened was too important to be forgotten. The story would remain part of the family's history only if it was passed on, just like his own. Miguel was part of the chain that could save his own family's story.

"How long were you at the school?" Miguel asked.

"Almost two hot seasons have passed," Rushing Cloud said. *Two years*, Miguel realized. "It is almost time for the planting rains to fall again." Rushing Cloud pulled his fingers through his short hair. "When I return to the *rancheria* I will never let my hair be chopped again. It will grow as long as my memory."

"Why did you finally run away?" Miguel asked.

"One morning the mission teachers carried white shirts for the boys to wear. They tell us every child will have his image made with the exploding box. They smile with their teeth, but we are afraid and wonder how we can get away before it is too late."

"Why?" Miguel asked. "There's nothing to be afraid of having your photograph taken." His family had once had a portrait made by a traveling photographer who came into Tucson. Miguel's mother placed the photograph in a glass-covered frame and hung it on the wall.

"Remember I say that my grandmother shared some wisdom before I was taken away?" Rushing Cloud asked. "She tells me that if the white man's flashing machine captures your image, your life will be short. She makes me promise I will not let them steal my old age."

Miguel had never heard anyone worry about being photographed. Still, Rushing Cloud's grandmother believed it, and so did he. "Couldn't you just tell the missionaries not to photograph you?"

Rushing Cloud grunted. "These elders do not listen to the voices of the young. In secret, I beg my cousins to come away with me, but they are too afraid. Others have run many times before, and we see how they are caught and chained with iron and given no food." His voice grew softer. "I know they can never catch me. In the night, I slip from the sleeping room. Outside, I put the white man's boots on backward and walk until I disappear."

The thought of Rushing Cloud using the Apache trick to hide his tracks made Miguel smile. He imagined the missionaries following Rushing Cloud's footprints from the desert into the building and searching under every bed and in every wardrobe. The two boys rolled to face each other and burst out laughing.

Suddenly, Rushing Cloud's expression grew serious. "I worry about my cousins. Maybe their lives will be too short. When they leave the white man's school, will they be able to live with their people again if they forget the old ways? That is why I must go home—back to the blanket. I must get there, my friend, before I lose more than I can find again."

Miguel closed his eyes. Before sleep closed his thoughts, an idea arose in his mind. *I am ready to go back to the blanket too. It is time for me to learn the old ways.*

When Miguel awoke in the shelter, he heard Rushing Cloud chanting, his voice floating on the evening air like a singing ghost. This would be their third night traveling together, and Miguel was thankful that he wouldn't be alone in the desert again.

He propped himself up on his elbow and looked toward the spot where the roadrunner had perched. Just beyond, Rushing Cloud sat in the same cross-legged position Miguel had seen before, facing the long clouds that stretched across the pink and violet light of the setting sun.

By the time his companion returned to the shelter, Miguel had taken down most of the branches. Together, they brushed over their footprints and began to walk. Miguel was still limping, but there was less pain now and he kept pace with Rushing Cloud.

Miguel felt a pang of guilt. He should have told his friend the truth about why he had become lost so far from his own home. He had to be honest. Miguel's mouth went dry.

"There's something—something I haven't told you," he stammered. "I—I did run away, away from my family."

"I know this—here," Rushing Cloud said, touching his heart. "I know because you never talk of your people. Yet you are thinking of them much of the time. Is it not so?"

"My father shared a story with me the night I left," Miguel began. "It was written in a book by an elder who lived long ago. He had been captured and brought to this land as a prisoner. In the book he told how the church had tried to force our ancestors to accept their faith—the one my family follows now! Many of the family, and so many others, were killed for following their own beliefs. Their land was taken from them."

Rushing Cloud nodded. "This is how my people lose their lands and are made to pray to a different god." He seemed to search Miguel's face for some sign of understanding. "We have shared our lives, my friend, although we have walked different paths."

Miguel was startled at the truth of Rushing Cloud's words. His ancestors—and Miguel's—had fought for the right to remain on their land and keep their own beliefs. Yet Miguel had wanted to become a priest and wipe out the beliefs of natives like Rushing Cloud. A hollow feeling settled in his chest. He didn't know if he could still think of following in Father Ignacio's footsteps. When he had rushed from the house, his faith was firm. Now he was filled with doubts.

"I didn't want to believe that my family was different than what I had always thought," Miguel declared. "It scared me to hear what had happened to my ancestors under the laws of my own church. I couldn't bear to listen! In just a few minutes, everything in my life changed—who I am, and who I thought I would become. I wanted my life to go back to the way it was before my father told that story—and I just ran. I never thought I would get so lost."

Rushing Cloud gazed toward the horizon. "So, you escape twice. Once from your ancestor's words, and again from Apachu who would change your life again. I think you are still the same inside—you are Miguel. Ancestors speak to us in many ways. You must only listen to know who you are."

Rushing Cloud pointed to a cluster of spiny barrel cactus nestled at the foot of a spindly mesquite tree. "Can you see that we are traveling home?" he asked. "The cactus points the way. I'itoi, the Creator, tells them to bend toward the sun so the Desert People will never be lost."

Miguel saw that the barrel cactus tilted slightly in one direction. "They must point south," he marveled. He had seen such cactus a thousand times, yet never noticed how they grew. With Rushing Cloud at his side, it was as if he were learning to see the desert for the first time. Rushing Cloud was passing along the traditions of his elders as if Miguel would also keep them from being forgotten.

Miguel wondered if Aharon ben Avraham had truly changed his religious beliefs when he came to this new land. Had he simply hidden them so long they had been lost between one generation and the next? Rushing Cloud was certain that neither Miguel nor his family had changed deep in their hearts. His friend's words settled into Miguel's thoughts and rested there.

Perhaps Miguel could remain strong in his Catholic faith and still honor the memory of his ancestor's life. Maybe the story of this ancient relative was God's way of showing Miguel that each person had to make his own choices. There were many paths before him, and Miguel had to choose the one he would follow. It was far more difficult than finding his way across the desert, but he thought that he was coming closer to the right path.

After they had traveled a short distance, Rushing Cloud pointed to a deep circular depression in the sand. "When the rains come, this *charco* will fill with water." He walked around the dry wash until he spotted a faint channel leading away from it. "Look, my friend. Here is where the water flows in from the mountain. We must find its mouth."

The trail led into the foothills, where grasses and low bushes grew in abundance. Rushing Cloud pulled up some of the greens and fastened them under his belt.

Miguel sniffed the air. "Onions!" he said.

Rushing Cloud nodded. "When we stop, we can roast them."

If there were onions growing, there had to be water nearby, Miguel thought. He bent low, parting the grasses as he went. The sand looked damp as he moved higher between the boulders. A faint trickle darkened a small rock, and a little farther ahead, Miguel found its source. A spring bubbled between a jumble of stones. "Water!" he called.

"Your eyes are open today, my friend," Rushing

Cloud said. Miguel captured a handful of the precious liquid, but when he drank his mouth filled with as much sand as water. He spit into the dirt.

Rushing Cloud laughed softly. He filled his gourd dipper with water, wrapped the edge of his shirt around it, and drank through the cloth. He rinsed out the wet sand that remained and handed his gourd and his shirt to Miguel. They each drank their fill and then traveled back down the slope in the deepening night. The silhouettes of giant saguaro stood out against the moonlight, their waxy white buds lit with a ghostly glow.

"Before long the saguaro fruit will ripen," Rushing Cloud observed, craning his neck to look at the luminous flowers. "Then my village will move their spring camps to gather them."

"Are the saguaro fruit good to eat?" Miguel asked.

"Yes. The women and girls strike the fruit with long sticks until they fall. Then the grandmothers cook them into syrup." His voice held a hint of excitement. "Everyone fills their *ollas*, and at home we mix the syrup with water to make a sweet drink. Every family offers a few jugs to the Keeper of the Smoke. He lets the syrup ripen. When it is ready, we drink and sing songs to call the rain. On the fourth day, thunder announces the season of growing. Black clouds fly across the sky, and rain comes to water our fields. The *charcos* fill." Rushing Cloud put his hand on Miguel's shoulder. "My mother tells that I came with the summer rains. She looked to the sky and saw the clouds rushing to give us water just as I came into this life. That is why I am called Rushing Cloud."

Miguel loved the time of year when thunderstorms washed the desert and the scent of creosote bushes filled the air. The ranch hands set rain barrels outside to hold the bounty of water, and the horse troughs overflowed.

"I will tell you something," Rushing Cloud confided. "If the Tohono O'odham do not sing up the rain, the desert will always be dry."

A new realization filled Miguel's head. Rushing Cloud may have learned to speak like a white man, but that hadn't changed his beliefs. His faith had shaken Miguel's.

He had always believed Father Ignacio when the priest declared that Indians were heathens who knew nothing about God or civilized life. He realized now that Father Ignacio could be mistaken. It could be true that Rushing Cloud's god brought the rains.

The Desert People might teach the settlers many things, if only they would listen. Rushing Cloud had already taught Miguel more in a short time than he ever imagined was possible.

The slope of the mountain range grew lower, and Miguel sensed they were getting closer to Tucson. A chill crept into the night air, but he wasn't cold, even without a shirt or shoes. Tonight he had walked several miles and he was still at Rushing Cloud's side, neither tired nor thirsty. Light from the sky lit his path. *I am more like the scorpion every day*, he thought, *finding my way through the dark.*

In the distance, Miguel thought he saw fires glowing. Was it an illusion of stars dancing in the desert? As he walked ahead, he realized it was the flickering of campfires! His heart raced.

"Enemy soldiers," Rushing Cloud announced, standing stock-still. The faint echo of laughter drifted across the still air.

"It's the cavalry," Miguel nearly shouted. He rushed forward, forgetting his tender foot. Rushing Cloud grabbed his arm roughly and pulled him back.

"You must wait until daylight, my friend. These warriors shoot their fire sticks at anything that rustles in the night."

Miguel tried to pull away. "Don't you understand? They're searching for me," he argued. "They wouldn't shoot!"

"Look at you," Rushing Cloud declared. "Your hair hangs down, and you wear a headband like Apachu. You have no shirt or boots, and your skin is dark from the sun and covered with red dust. How can you think of running into their camp? They will not know you."

Miguel slumped down in the sand and pulled the strip of cloth from his head. He had waited so long to be rescued, and now he would have to wait even longer.

"Maybe they won't believe me when I tell them who I am," he said. "Maybe they'll think I'm their enemy."

"Come," Rushing Cloud said in his soft voice. He moved toward the boulders to the west. "We will go closer, but we will stay in the shadow of the mountain. Tomorrow, when the sun shines upon you, call out to them and enter their camp in safety. I will follow and watch to make sure they take you home. After all, we still travel the same path." He handed Miguel his shirt. "Wear this," he said.

Miguel pulled the shirt over his head, struggling

to ease it over the sling. Pain throbbed in his shoulder with the slightest touch.

"You're right," he admitted. "You probably saved my life again just now. I would have run into the camp and startled the sentries. Tomorrow we'll go in together, and this time, I'll be able to help you. I'll tell the soldiers what you did for me. I won't let them take you back to the mission school, I promise. Maybe they'll give you a horse so you can get back to your family quicker. Agreed?"

He poked his head through the opening in the shirt and tugged it into place. The fabric felt strange against his bare skin, and he almost wished to feel the air against his chest again. He looked up when his companion didn't answer, but Rushing Cloud was gone.

CHAPTER 13
Grizzled Eggs and Rio Coffee

Miguel huddled against the rocks. He squinted into the inky night, hoping that Rushing Cloud would return as suddenly as he had disappeared. He longed to hear the comforting sound of his friend's voice singing up the dawn. When at last the sun eased over the horizon in a halo of orange light, Miguel knew Rushing Cloud was not coming back.

The shadow of a lone buzzard glided across the sand, and Miguel looked up to watch the bird's dark wings floating effortlessly. The ranch hands called the bird *zopilote*, and said it knew every inch of its territory. The desert was Rushing Cloud's territory, and Miguel was certain that his friend would navigate his way home as silently as the bird's shadow.

Miguel stood and stretched, his muscles stiff from

sitting in the cold. His shoulder throbbed with pain, and his mouth was parched. He had gotten used to walking at night and now he needed sleep. But the only thing that mattered was getting home. He'd walk into the cavalry encampment and let them take him the rest of the way. His time in the desert was almost over.

As the sun rose higher, Miguel spotted a sentry posted on a stand of low rocks. The guard stood out clearly against the brightening sky. *If I were an Apache, that soldier would be an easy target.*

Taking a few steps forward, Miguel cupped his hand around his mouth and yelled a greeting. "Ho, there!" Although his injured foot prevented him from running, he moved closer at a steady pace and the distance between him and the guard shortened. The startled sentry raised his rifle in Miguel's direction.

Miguel stopped. "Don't shoot!" he called.

Without lowering his rifle, the guard shouted back across the open expanse. "Identify yourself!" His deep voice echoed off the rocks, and Miguel heard the faint repetition of the last word until it faded away. "Yourself . . . your . . . self . . ."

"I'm lost," Miguel called. "I'm trying to get back to Tucson."

Two more armed soldiers scrambled onto the rocks, crouching down on either side of the sentry. Now three rifles aimed at Miguel's chest. Perhaps Rushing Cloud had been right to leave. How would the guards have reacted to two strangers approaching their camp?

"Approach slowly," the guard ordered gruffly.

Miguel thought he should raise his hands over his head to show he was unarmed, but that wasn't possible with his injured shoulder. He might look more dangerous with one arm in the air. He exaggerated his limp, dragging his leg more than necessary so that he wouldn't appear threatening. Still, the soldiers didn't lower their guns.

At close range, the men eyed him warily. They stood together, their tall crowned hats pinned up on the right side and a small white plume decorating the left. It seemed a strange and useless hat to wear while riding across the desert and even stranger during guard duty. The feathery plume alone would signal a soldier's hiding place. One young soldier, whose burly neck seemed choked by his tight blue wool jacket, shaded his eyes with his hand and scanned the desert as if there might be others hiding in wait.

"Identify yourself!" the sentry demanded again. Like his companions, his baggy blue trousers were tucked into tall leather boots folded over at the knees. Their square toes looked hard and sturdy. Miguel looked down at his dirty feet, covered with scratches and angry cuts. He couldn't help thinking how his boots would have protected him from the scorpion's sting.

Being stung had prevented Miguel from continuing on his own, but it had brought Rushing Cloud to help him. Miguel didn't know if he had gained any special qualities from the scorpion, but walking the desert with Rushing Cloud at his side had given Miguel a chance to see everything around him in a different way. He had learned that the desert could provide food and water. He had seen how to survive. He had found time to think.

Miguel looked squarely at the guard. "My name is Miguel," he said. "My father is Don Mateo Abrano. We have a horse ranch just outside Tucson."

"Well, I'll be hog-tied," the sentry declared, finally dropping the rifle to his side. He turned to one of the other soldiers. "Go tell Captain we found the kid." The messenger clambered down the rocks and rushed into the camp, his hat plume bobbing.

"We gave you up for dead, boy," said one of the remaining soldiers. He put a strong arm around Miguel and supported him as they entered the cluster of tents and smoldering campfires. Groggy soldiers still in their long underwear stumbled from their low white tents to watch him pass.

The camp tents stretched in parallel rows, giving Miguel the feeling that he was walking down a narrow street. Wispy smoke wafted from the remains of last night's cooking fires like snuffed beacons. In the center of the camp, horses were tethered to wooden stakes driven into the ground. Some of the animals lifted their heads and tossed their long manes. Miguel was sure they had been purchased from his family's stock. Abrano horses were direct descendants of the mounts used by the Spanish conquistadors, and they seemed to carry themselves with a fierce pride, as if they knew their lineage.

Miguel had felt a sense of pride about his family's heritage too. Now doubts had seeped into his mind. He had to admit that Aharon ben Avraham had shown tremendous courage in spite of all that had happened to him. He had tried to keep his faith, even when faced with death. He had overcome great tragedy to build a new life, passing on his beliefs at great risk.

If the scorpion can share his strengths through his sting, Miguel thought, *couldn't my ancestor's story give me the courage see my own life in a new way?*

The row of tents ended at a covered supply wagon that created a barricade. "Wait here," ordered the soldier who had helped Miguel into camp. He entered a tent set up at the end of the line. It was far larger than the others, and a canopy extended from the front.

The tent wasn't nearly as interesting as the food cooking nearby. A gray-haired soldier leaned over a black iron frying pan, and Miguel's mouth watered at the smell of sizzling bacon. A barrel of water sat atop the wagon back, and a few drops dripped from a wooden spigot. Miguel was about to ask for a drink when the cook and the soldiers nearby suddenly snapped to attention and gave a stiff salute as a tall, barrel-chested man stepped out of the tent. Miguel thought the man's shoulder patches identified him as an officer, but if not, his crisp uniform and ramrod posture certainly did.

"Come in, son," he said, holding the tent flap open. "I'm Captain Riverton." He stepped inside behind Miguel and addressed the guard. "Fetch the medic," he ordered, and the soldier hurried away.

The tent was high enough for Miguel and the captain to stand comfortably. It was sparsely furnished with a wooden table and two low stools, a leather trunk, and a cot whose blankets were pulled taut. The captain pointed to one of the three-legged stools, and Miguel sat down, grateful to rest his foot.

"I don't know how you arrived here," the captain marveled. "We tracked you to a cottonwood stand, but then we lost your trail. Our scout guessed that you had been taken by Apache, and he knew their tricks. We picked up the trail again heading into the mountains and thought we'd catch up with you in a day or two, but then the trail went cold. We searched for two more days and, finally, gave you up for lost." The captain smiled. "It's been a full nine days now, and here you are! You've shown us all up for fools by finding us, instead of us finding you. You're a pretty resourceful chap to escape from a band of Apaches and make your way across the desert alone."

"I wasn't alone," Miguel blurted out. "You see, I—"

"Breakfast, sir," the cook interrupted, setting two plates of steaming food on the worn tabletop. Miguel stared at the fried eggs, crisp bacon, and pan biscuits heaped on each plate. He picked up the fork that was stabbed into the biscuit and felt his hand trembling. Everything felt strange and different, even holding a fork. The aroma of the food made Miguel realize how desperately hungry he was. The cook carefully set two mugs of steaming coffee beside the plates and left.

"Grizzled eggs and Rio coffee," the captain declared. "Not much of a welcome home meal, but I reckon your mother will remedy that soon enough." Miguel was so thirsty that he took a deep swallow of the coffee and shuddered at its bitterness. "There's no room for luxuries like sugar on the trail," the captain apologized in a voice loud enough for the soldiers outside to hear. Then, with a wink, he quietly retrieved a small metal canister from his trunk and poured a stream of coarse brown sugar into each of their cups. He buried the canister under a shirt in the trunk and closed the lid.

"So," the captain said in a friendly manner, "I'm interested to hear that you had some help on the way back." His smile seemed frozen. "Who were you with out there?"

CHAPTER 14
A Rebel Yell

Miguel chewed a mouthful of bacon, savoring the smoky taste. "Well, I was alone some of the time," he said. "When I first got away, that is." The captain looked puzzled. "The Apache brought me pretty far up into the Catalina Mountains," Miguel explained, "and there was no chance to escape. Then one night there was a real ruckus and I made a run for it. I nearly got away, but a warrior hit me with a stick and I tumbled over the side of a bluff. That's when I got this cut on my head, and my shoulder got hurt pretty bad. By the time I landed on the ground I was covered in cactus thorns. Even though I was so banged up, I knew I had to keep moving before the Apaches found me again. I tried to walk south and travel mostly at night so they wouldn't see me.

I slept during the day when it was hot." His words tumbled out. "I didn't have any food or water. Then I stepped on a scorpion in the dark and lanced my foot with my pocketknife to try to drain the poison." He looked down. "I guess that was pretty dumb."

The captain listened attentively, and Miguel stopped talking just long enough to gulp down another swallow of coffee. Even with sugar, its bitterness was powerful. "After that, I think I passed out for a while, and when I woke up, a boy about my age was leaning over me. He had pulled out most of the cactus spines and bandaged my head and foot. He had even cooked a rabbit and found some water." Miguel took a breath. "He seemed to know the way back to Tucson, and once I could move, we traveled together." Miguel mopped up the runny egg yolk with the last piece of biscuit. "If he hadn't helped me, I would have died out there."

A clean-shaven young soldier with ruddy cheeks pulled back the tent flap and stepped in. "Medic, sir!" he said, saluting. He held a pail of water in one hand and had a leather haversack slung over his shoulder.

"Corporal Pinter," the captain greeted him, "this here's the young chap who took a little sojourn with the Apaches. Here he is back from the dead to haunt us." The two men shared a short laugh. The captain looked at Miguel's empty plate. "You had enough?"

Miguel nodded. "Thank you, sir."

Then the captain noticed the half-filled coffee mug. "I know you've had enough of that. In fact, I think I see hair sprouting on your chest already."

The medic grinned. "That Rio coffee'll grow hair on a bald man," he said. Then he looked flustered. "No offense, sir," he stammered.

"Check over this desert rat, will you, Corporal?" the captain said. "He's been clubbed by Apaches, fallen over a cliff, and been bit by a scorpion, but here he sits."

The medic took a clean cloth and a sliver of brown soap from the bucket and washed the dirt from around the wound on Miguel's forehead.

"This seems to be healing nicely," the corporal said. "Now let's see what's under that bandage on your foot. If you can call it a bandage!" He peeled off the soiled strip of fabric. "Stung by a scorpion, eh? Nasty little devils."

Miguel looked at the angry red skin that swelled around the cut. He spoke softly to the medic. "My friend Rushing Cloud said the scorpion was giving me a message to be more like him—to drink very little water, to travel at night, and to navigate by the stars."

The captain interrupted. "Miguel was telling me that after he was stung by the scorpion a boy found him and led him across the desert." He looked at Miguel. "An Indian boy, I presume?"

"He's a Tohono O'odham," Miguel corrected him as the medic prodded the tender flesh around the cut. "He's nothing like the Apache."

"*Tono* . . . what?" the corporal asked. "I've never heard of any tribe called that. Only friendly Indians I've ever seen were Papagos."

Miguel spoke up again, eager to share his new knowledge. "Papago is what some people call the Tohono O'odham, but they don't like it one bit. Their real name means People of the Desert."

"Mighty interesting," said the medic.

Miguel winced as the medic cleaned the wound. "I never knew what the word *Papago* meant, and I sure didn't know it was kind of an insult. You know what else? The Apache don't like the name *Apache*, either. It means 'enemy,' so it makes them angry. They call themselves Indé."

And what should I be called? Miguel suddenly

thought with confusion. He was Mexican, but when Mexico sold the territory where the family had its ranch, he became American—just like magic. He remembered Rushing Cloud saying that while people might change on the outside, they are still the same on the inside, where it counts. Miguel was American, but he would always have his Mexican heritage.

"So where is this Indian of yours?" the captain asked, interrupting Miguel's thoughts.

Miguel felt an unexplained emptiness. "His name is Rushing Cloud," he repeated. "He disappeared last night after we found your camp. I wanted him to stay with me. I told him the cavalry would help him get home too, but he just vanished."

Miguel glanced up just as the captain and the medic exchanged a meaningful look. A feeling of uneasiness settled over Miguel, and he eyed the men warily.

"Luckily, these wounds are pretty clean," the medic said, packing up his bag. "You're going to have a couple of right manly scars there, though. Someday you can brag to your grandchildren about how you got them."

The burst of energy that had fueled Miguel's flood of conversation was nearly spent. He felt consumed by exhaustion and couldn't keep his eyes from fluttering closed.

"I know you're plumb worn out," the corporal said, "but I'm gonna have to take a closer look at that shoulder. Can you take off your shirt?"

"It's really Rushing Cloud's," Miguel explained. "He gave it to me last night." He tried to pull it off, but couldn't raise his arm high enough. The medic gently slid the sleeve from Miguel's good arm and eased the shirt over his head. Next, he untied the sling. Miguel groaned as the young soldier tested how far the arm could move and then prodded the joint with his fingers. Searing pain surged through Miguel's shoulder and spread across his chest and back.

The medic let out a breath. "This arm is pulled right out of its socket. I can pop it back in, and it'll likely heal just fine, but it's going to wake you up real good when I yank it."

The captain stepped quietly outside the tent, his boot steps moving off down the row of tents and sounding fainter and fainter. The sound of tin plates and cups rattled in Miguel's ears, and the soldiers' voices seemed louder than they had before.

"I usually give the men a couple of shots of whiskey before I perform this little maneuver," the corporal said, taking a dented metal flask from his sack. "I guess if you're old enough to be clubbed by an Apache, you're man enough for a swig of this to help you through."

"I just turned thirteen," Miguel murmured. He had believed it when Papá had told him he would become a man when he had his birthday. Yet he had felt like a child compared to the Apache and like a bumbling little brother next to Rushing Cloud.

Miguel sniffed the amber liquid in the flask. It gave off a woody aroma mingled with a faint hint of sweetness, but both were overpowered by a sharp, pungent smell.

"I don't know," he said slowly. "I guess I could give it a try."

"Just swig it," Corporal Pinter advised. "If you let that whiskey linger in your mouth, you'll never get it down." He looked apologetic. "I wouldn't give this to you if there was a better way."

Miguel's hand shook as he lifted the flask and gulped down a large swallow of whiskey. He coughed and sputtered as the fiery drink burned his throat and lit into his stomach like a burning match. He tried to hand the container back, but instead, the corporal tilted Miguel's head back and forced him to drink more. He gagged on the fiery liquid.

"Everybody remembers their first shot of whiskey," the medic said, releasing Miguel. "Just add this to that list of stories you'll have to tell." He helped Miguel over to the captain's cot and eased him down onto his back. The wooden frame creaked, and the thin mattress sagged under him. Miguel had not seen a soft bed piled with wool blankets in weeks, and he longed to give in to the need for sleep. His head felt light, and the room began to float in a hazy blur of images.

"Go ahead," the medic's voice soothed. "Just let go." Miguel tried to focus on the soldier's face, but it dissolved into a pink shadow. He closed his eyes, but the room still seemed to be spinning. The medic straightened Miguel's arm, and he gasped at the pain.

"You ever heard a rebel yell?" the corporal asked, but Miguel couldn't focus on the question and his tongue felt thick and unable to form words. The medic kept talking in gentle tones, as if from a great distance, and slivers of pain darted through Miguel's shoulder like arrows. "Guess you're not old enough for that. During the war I unfortunately had occasion to hear them Southern Rebs give their famous yell. Why, it just curdled my blood. Lucky you never heard it for yourself. But you think on it, and when I fix to pull this shoulder back into place, you give it a try. Just yell for all you're worth. I bet you'll come real close."

The medic braced his knee on Miguel's chest, and Miguel's eyes fluttered open for a moment. One thick hand pressed around his shoulder at the joint, and the other gripped his upper arm. He wanted to see what the medic was doing, but he was overcome with dizziness. Suddenly, Miguel's shoulder seemed to rip from his body with a sickening *pop!* In a blinding flash of white light that blazed across his closed eyelids, Miguel heard a distant voice let out a wild, deafening scream.

CHAPTER 15
Indian Prisoner

A clamor of unfamiliar noises disturbed Miguel's heavy sleep. He awoke to the stifling heat of the captain's tent, illuminated by bright sunlight against the canvas roof. His head throbbed from the clatter of pots, cursing soldiers, and wagon wheels creaking and groaning. He struggled to his feet, holding the tent pole for support.

Miguel's stomach roiled and a sour taste, like rancid butter, rose in his throat. Lurching through the tent flaps, he fell onto his knees, vomiting until his stomach had given up every bit of breakfast.

"Considerate of you not to foul the captain's quarters." Miguel tried to focus on the tall boots planted in front of his face, then raised his eyes to meet those of the medic. Corporal Pinter reached down and helped Miguel to stand. Everything around him seemed to tilt from one side to another, and his stomach felt queasy.

"I told you no one ever forgets his first taste of whiskey," the medic said with a wry smile. "How's that shoulder?"

Miguel tried to move his arm, but a stiff canvas sling bound his shoulder tightly against his side. His elbow was fixed in a bent position, and he could barely wiggle his fingers. Sharp pains in his shoulder throbbed in time with a pulsating headache. Miguel opened his mouth to answer, but he couldn't seem to speak.

"You're a pale shade of green," the corporal said. "Better sit down." He led Miguel back into the tent and settled him on the cot. "Camp's just about broke and we'll still make a few miles today. Think you can handle a wagon ride?" When Miguel nodded his agreement, a new wave of dizziness washed over him.

"Drop your head between your knees," Corporal Pinter said. Miguel leaned over, and the lightheadedness began to ease.

The medic kept talking quietly. "I'm sorry to report that we won't make it back to Tucson today. We already lost most of the morning because we didn't want to move you too soon." He eased Miguel into Rushing Cloud's shirt. "The captain sent a messenger on ahead, though, so when we arrive tomorrow, you'll get a proper welcome." The corporal opened the lid on a wooden bucket filled with water and dipped in a tin mug. He handed it to Miguel. "Some water will help clear your head."

Miguel took a few sips, and the medic splashed the remaining water onto the dirt floor. Miguel's heart raced as he watched the water soak into the dry earth, but he was too worn out to utter a word of protest.

"Okay, *amigo*, it's roundup time," the corporal said. He helped Miguel out of the tent, supporting him with one strong arm. Two sweating cavalrymen began dismantling the tent, pulling up the stakes and rolling the ropes. As Miguel moved away, he saw the aide dump out all the water that remained in the bucket.

The camp seemed swallowed up in a confusion of rushing soldiers. Men tied their tents and haversacks onto their horses and hung frying pans and tin cups from their bulging saddlebags. Several cavalrymen kicked sand over the smoking ashes from abandoned campfires. A few broken tent stakes littered the ground, and one soldier scraped the remains from a dirty plate onto a pile of rotting garbage. The shallow latrine was hastily covered with a few shovelfuls of sand. Miguel stepped carefully around horse droppings that dotted the area where the animals had been tethered, painfully aware of his bare, unprotected feet.

Wagons and horses lined up as they were ready, and the corporal guided Miguel directly to the cook wagon at the front. Three-legged iron pots were stacked inside atop sacks of flour and beans. The water barrel was attached to the back.

"Cookie will take good care of you," said the medic. The cook who had served up breakfast a few hours earlier gave Miguel a two-fingered salute. He sported a clean shave, and his uniform was neatly brushed.

"You hungry, son?" he asked.

Miguel shook his head gingerly. His attention was drawn to a slow drip coming from the spigot on the water barrel. He cleared his throat and pointed at the barrel.

"You're losing water," he said, his voice raspy.

"Don't pay it no mind," the cook reassured him. "We've got enough water to float this cavalry back to Tucson."

"Careful with that shoulder," the medic warned the cook. The two men lifted Miguel onto the wagon seat in one swift motion. Corporal Pinter looked up at Miguel and winked. "No bronco busting or cattle roping today. I'll check on you again after we set camp tonight."

Miguel managed a weak smile. "I guess I will take it easy," he said, "since my head feels like it's been hit with a fence post and my shoulder feels like it's on fire. But I'm almost home."

He looked toward the horizon. If Rushing Cloud was watching, he would see that Miguel was safe. Miguel prayed that his friend was making his own way home.

The cook swung up onto the wagon seat and took the reins of the mule team in his callused hands. Miguel couldn't stop thinking about the leaking water. The bucket from the captain's tent that had already been wasted that morning would have been enough to last him and Rushing Cloud for days. *Just like the scorpion*, Miguel thought.

Miguel turned and watched the campsite fall away behind him. There wasn't so much as a patch of sagebrush left where the tents had been pitched. An empty burlap flour sack settled into the dust, the red letters stamped on it already faded.

It seemed that the soldiers were determined to change everything around them, leaving nothing as they had found it. Rushing Cloud and the band of Apaches were content to be part of the desert, accepting what it had to offer and leaving no trace behind.

Instead of the near silence that had engulfed Miguel as the warriors moved along a trail, the army officers continually shouted orders, and the clattering wagons made a constant din. Miguel missed the soothing sound of Rushing Cloud's prayerful singing.

In the late afternoon, as the shadows of the mule team lengthened, the captain rode along the line, barking out orders. The rattling procession drew to a halt. Mounted soldiers rode up to form a double line and dismounted.

"Are we stopping already?" Miguel asked. "There's plenty of daylight left."

Cookie whistled the mules to the end of the ragged line and pulled them to a halt. "It's a heap of work to settle these boys down for the night," he explained. "There's the horses to be tended, tents to be pitched, and food cooked up. It'll be dark before the last plate of beans disappears."

Now that Miguel was so close to home, a lump rose in his throat at the thought of seeing his parents again. He was ashamed to face them and at the same time realized how much he missed them. He hoped he would be able to find the words to make them understand how the past days had changed him. He felt as if the boy Miguel had walked and walked until he disappeared.

Rushing Cloud would say that Miguel was still the same inside, but now he saw everything around him with new eyes. When Miguel first heard the opening pages of the diary, he had felt anger and shame. Now he had a sense of calm and a willingness to listen.

"Come on," Cookie said, helping Miguel down from the wagon. "Find yourself a spot out of the way, and I'll fix you some supper along with the captain's." He chuckled. "That means your beans get some salt pork in them."

Miguel leaned against the wagon wheel and watched the cook stoke a fire and hang black pots of beans from an iron frame. All the soldiers were busy with their own chores and started their own cooking fires. Through the smoky haze, the camp rose out of the desert like a mirage. Men lined up at the water barrel, and Miguel cringed as water splashed into the sand each time the spigot opened or closed.

After the cook had served the captain his dinner, he filled two more plates and balanced one on Miguel's lap. Miguel scooped up the spicy beans with pieces of blackened corn bread.

Cookie looked at the burnt edges of the pale yellow bread. "May not be perfect," he said, "but it sure beats hardtack."

"It tastes good to me," Miguel said. "It's a heap better than an empty stomach and lots better than horsemeat."

"I can't figure how those Indians can eat a horse." Cookie spit into the sand. "They're savages." Miguel was startled by the cook's hateful words.

"I guess it's all a matter of what you're used to," he said carefully. "My friend Rushing Cloud said that at the mission school, the native kids hated the food. They weren't used to it, and it made them sick." The cook grunted. Before his journey, Miguel might have accepted Cookie's opinion, but not anymore. The Apache ate what was available, and they were satisfied with little.

Miguel thought of how easily Jacob Franck accepted people who were different from him. The peddler accepted the native people and got along with them. He hadn't tried to convince the Abranos that his religion was better, or that anyone had to accept his faith to be his friend. It was Miguel who had felt the need to convert nonbelievers in order to accept them.

Miguel shouldn't have judged Señor Franck so quickly. The way the peddler dressed or wore his beard didn't make him a demon. Neither did his prayers, simply because they sounded strange to Miguel.

Miguel was restless after sitting on the wagon for so long. That night he wandered around the camp. Tough new skin had grown over the soles of his feet, and he forgot that he had no boots. He looked around the campsite, trying to take his mind off the throbbing pain in his shoulder. He hoped the medic knew what he was doing.

A small group of cavalrymen sat around a small fire while one soldier played a lively tune on a harmonica. They beckoned to him, and Miguel stood at the edge of the ragged circle. The men clapped and hummed along until the harmonica player took a break, wiping off the silver instrument with his neck scarf. Some of the men rolled cigarettes, and one offered Miguel a mug of coffee.

"No, thanks," he said. "My stomach isn't sure what it wants to do with the beans and corn bread I just ate. If I add that Rio coffee, I'm afraid it's going to decide it doesn't want any of it!"

The men chuckled. The harmonica player lifted the instrument back to his lips, and Miguel recognized the song. Some of the men started to sing the words to "Shenandoah." The song was filled with longing, and Miguel felt more homesick than ever. He was so close to home, and yet it seemed so far off.

Suddenly, there was a commotion at the far end of camp. A cavalryman rode in as a crowd of soldiers swarmed around. In the flickering firelight, Miguel saw that the rider was leading a bare-chested Indian. His hands were tied in front of him, and he was tethered to the saddle horn with a long rope. Miguel stretched to get a better look, and the queasy feeling in the pit of his stomach came roiling back. Even from a distance, he knew that the prisoner was Rushing Cloud.

Miguel tried to push through the crush of men. "Rushing Cloud!" he called, but his friend stared straight ahead. He was bruised and dirty, as if he'd been in a scuffle. The mounted soldier drew to a halt in front of the captain, who was seated on a stool outside his tent, puffing on a clay pipe.

The soldier dismounted and stood at attention, giving the captain a crisp salute. "I knew you said there might be an Indian following the Abrano boy, sir, so I kept my eyes open. I found this one sneaking behind some bushes while I was patrolling the perimeter. I think he's an Apache scout."

The captain rose from his chair. "Beef up the guard," he said to his aide. "If he's one of the warriors that had captured Don Mateo's son, he won't be alone." The aide moved down the line, calling out certain men by name.

Miguel pushed into the clearing in front of the tent. "He's no Apache," he blurted out. "He's my friend, Rushing Cloud. Untie him!"

The captain scowled. "I think the whiskey is still affecting your judgment, so I'm willing to excuse your interference this time. Don't let it happen again."

"But Captain Riverton, this is the person who saved me out in the desert. I told you about him, remember? How can he be an Apache, when he's wearing sandals instead of moccasins? Look at his hair—it's short! He's wearing pants like you and me! No Apache warrior would be traveling without a double quiver of arrows and a bow. And he speaks perfect English!" Miguel faced his friend. "Talk to him, Rushing Cloud." Miguel's plea was ignored. Rushing Cloud remained silent, staring straight ahead.

"Set up the cage," the captain ordered, "and see that his hands and feet are tied. I'll deal with him in the morning." There was a flurry of sharp salutes from the soldiers as Rushing Cloud was led roughly away.

"Don't hurt him!" Miguel shouted. He turned to the captain and felt all the strength leave his body. "He saved my life," he said, his voice sounding like a whimper. "He's my friend."

"Get some sleep, son," Captain Riverton said sternly. "You've got a lot to learn about Indians."

CHAPTER 16
A Vanishing Trail

Miguel squatted in the sand behind the captain's tent trying to hear the conversation inside. The soldiers had drifted back to their tents after the commotion over Rushing Cloud's capture. The camp was quiet as the men turned in for the night.

None of the voices filtering through the canvas walls sounded familiar, but Miguel could hear enough to know they were discussing Rushing Cloud. Why hadn't the captain believed Miguel? After all, he knew who had captured him—not the soldiers. The longer the officers debated what to do with Rushing Cloud, the more Miguel worried.

A deep, raspy voice spoke out forcefully. "We can't risk taking that redskin into Tucson! If there's a band of Apaches trying to rescue him, we'll be attacked before we make it back. I say we shoot him now and leave his carcass for the buzzards." Miguel was stricken with fear until he heard Captain Riverton's commanding voice.

"We don't kill anyone unless they've gotten a fair trial and been proven guilty of a crime," the captain declared.

Someone else spoke up. "Why would the Abrano boy say the kid we captured was his friend if it weren't true?"

"I believe him, all right," Captain Riverton said. "That's why I told the watch that he might still be lurking around. I don't care if he's Apache or Papago. He can't be trusted."

Miguel was ashamed of his loose tongue. How foolish he had been to think an officer in the US Cavalry would believe a story about a friendly native. *If I had kept quiet, Rushing Cloud would never have been captured. It's all my fault.*

The three men inside the tent continued to debate whether to keep Rushing Cloud prisoner or execute him.

There was silence until the captain said, "I'll sleep on it. I'll see you both here at reveille and let you know what I've decided." Miguel heard the rustling of stiff uniforms and boot steps against the ground. He huddled closer to the back of the tent, pushing farther into the darkness.

Rushing Cloud's fate would be decided before dawn. Either he would be taken into Tucson as a prisoner or he would be shot before the cavalry pulled up stakes.

When he was sure the others had left, Miguel sneaked back to the cook wagon. No one had told him where to bed down for the night, but that meant no one was watching him. He was glad to be left alone. He needed time to think.

He clambered clumsily into the back of the wagon, wincing as his shoulder banged against the water barrel. He settled on a sack of cornmeal, massaging the muscles that throbbed from his neck all the way to his back. The only sound was of faint snoring from a nearby tent.

Miguel was tired too, but he couldn't sleep yet— not before he figured out how to save his friend. Until now, it had been Rushing Cloud who had made the decisions, always knowing the best way to stay safe. Now Miguel had to find the right path on his own, and it was more than simply finding his way home.

Slipping to the front of the wagon, he peered out across the driver's seat. There was little moonlight from the crescent that hung in the sky, but Miguel was used to traveling at night. His eyes adjusted to the darkness. The rows of white tents were easy to see, almost glowing under the brilliant stars.

First, Miguel had to figure out where they were holding Rushing Cloud. Captain Riverton had mentioned a cage. It would have to be large enough to hold a man, but small enough to be carried on one of the supply wagons. Miguel scanned the area beyond the tents. The latrines had been dug on the right side of camp, far enough from the cook wagon and the officers' tents, yet not so far that the men would be in danger when they used them. It wasn't likely that Rushing Cloud had been placed there.

To the left, Miguel barely made out shadowy giant saguaros reaching their branching arms toward the sky. Closer to the campsite he spotted a small red dot glowing and fading against the darkness. A cigarette! There must be a guard posted there. Miguel remembered the sentry he had approached yesterday morning, standing atop an outcropping of rock. Didn't these soldiers understand how they made themselves open targets? If Miguel could pick them out in the dark, an enemy scout could easily pick them off.

He cradled his bandaged arm tightly and eased himself from the wagon. His bare feet moved silently across the warm sand. Miguel stood as still as the saguaros, waiting to see if he had drawn anyone's attention. If a soldier questioned him, he would simply say he was looking for the latrine. They wouldn't think it suspicious that he was heading the wrong way in the dark.

Keeping his head low, Miguel crept in the direction of the guard's lit cigarette. It moved to the left, then to the right, as if floating in the air. *He's pacing back and forth, but staying in the same path*, he noted. That had to be where Rushing Cloud was imprisoned.

Several wooden barrels were stacked at the edge of camp, and Miguel crouched behind them. Just ahead, he saw the low, square shape of a wooden cage. It seemed too short for a person to stand inside, and barely wide enough for a prisoner to stretch out his arms. Miguel stared at the makeshift prison for several minutes before he noticed the shadowy shape of his friend curled on the ground.

Anger swelled in Miguel's chest at such cruel treatment, just because Rushing Cloud was an

Indian. He wanted to rush forward and free him, but he knew any sudden move would alert the sentry. Miguel had to be patient and think of the surest way to release his friend.

He watched the guard's measured steps until he was out of sight, then counted the seconds until the soldier retraced his steps . . . *sixty-eight, sixty-nine, seventy.* Miguel would have less than seventy seconds to get to the cage, cut an opening, and get away.

Miguel didn't see any other sentries, yet he was sure the captain would have placed extra men on watch. He sat motionless, scanning the area until he briefly glimpsed a light flare to his left. Almost immediately, the bright flame was extinguished, and Miguel saw the red glow of another cigarette pinpointing the location of another guard. How reckless these soldiers were! He followed the movement of the second sentry, marking the spot where their paths crossed.

As the soldiers retreated, Miguel pulled the jackknife from his pocket and opened the sharp blade. He approached the cage stealthily. Not every guard would be careless enough to announce his position with a lit cigarette. But Miguel saw no one except Rushing Cloud, curled on his side, asleep.

Although Miguel had moved silently, Rushing Cloud lifted his head as Miguel approached. They stared at each other through the wooden bars. Miguel began slicing through the thick cords that held the cage together when he heard a sentry returning. His boots thudded against the ground. Miguel flattened himself onto the sand, and Rushing Cloud curled up on his side, feigning sleep. *Had he really been asleep when I got here, or only pretending so the guards wouldn't watch him closely?*

Miguel had misjudged the timing of the soldiers' return. His heart pounded so hard he was afraid it was sending a drumbeat echoing across the desert. With the knife in his hand, Miguel knew he could never explain his presence if the guard discovered him there. He slipped the knife under a stake that tethered the cage to the ground.

Then he remembered the trick Rushing Cloud had taught him. He pulled the rattlesnake tail from his pocket. As the guard came closer, Miguel shook the rattles until they vibrated their threat. The sentry backed away.

Just then, a soft whistle cut the silence and the retreating guard returned the signal with his own low whistle. "I've got it," whispered a voice. Pale moonlight reflected off a silvery flask that the sentry held aloft. "He okay in there?"

"Sleeping like a baby," was the muffled reply, "in the company of a wide-awake rattler. The captain may not have to make any decisions by tomorrow. Let's get out of here." The two guards disappeared into the night.

Miguel didn't move for several seconds after the soldiers had left. He was uncertain where they would go. The area was flat, and only a few scrubby bushes dotted the area. When he was sure he heard and saw no signs of them, he retrieved his knife. With deft strokes, he cut out two wooden bars. Although Rushing Cloud's hands were tied together, he gripped each bar in his fingers and soundlessly placed them across each other in the center of the cage, as if marking the spot where he had been. Then he slid through the small opening on his belly.

Miguel cut the ropes that bound Rushing Cloud's wrists. As they fell away, he handed his friend the knife. Rushing Cloud slit the ropes that tied his ankles together and offered Miguel the folded knife.

"You keep the Snake Skinner," Miguel said in a voice as soft as Rushing Cloud's had been the first time he had spoken. As his friend tucked the pocketknife into his pants, Miguel pointed to Rushing Cloud's feet and whispered, "Give."

Rushing Cloud patted Miguel's back, understanding the joke and the message behind it. He removed his sandals and handed them to Miguel. Then he stood up, watching as Miguel tied the sandals onto his own feet, toes against heels.

In a barely audible voice, Rushing Cloud said, "Never again will you be a boy who wanders the desert without seeing. Remember me, Brother Scorpion." He laid one hand across his chest. "I am Rushing Cloud, son of Rain Stalker, son of I'itoi, creator of my people."

Miguel stood tall, his back ramrod straight. In a hushed, but strong voice, he said, "And remember me, my friend. I am Miguel, son of Mateo, son of Abraham, the father of my people." Rushing Cloud turned and loped across the desert like an antelope.

Miguel gathered the pieces of cut rope and used them to brush all tracks from around the cage. He hid the snake rattles deep in his pocket and then walked with heavy footsteps away from the empty prison. When he had traveled a good distance, he buried the sandals in a shallow hole and scattered stones and underbrush over it. He skirted the area, brushing his footprints from the sand behind him.

Despite his exhaustion, Miguel lay awake in the cook wagon, trying to sort out his jumbled thoughts. He understood Jacob Franck's hope that there would be more tolerance in Arizona, but Miguel realized how many differences remained. He had been just like so many in Tucson who thought that only their ways could be right.

The image of the peddler reading from his ancestor's diary flashed across his memory once again, but his thoughts had changed. Many things in his life now looked different. Getting back to his family would only be the start of a new journey.

Before his family's past was revealed, Miguel had only wanted to lead people to a belief in the church's teachings. Now, he knew he could never tell people like Rushing Cloud and Señor Franck that their beliefs were wrong. Who could know what songs God listened to?

He pictured Father Ignacio's sad face. Miguel would have to try to explain why he no longer believed he should become a priest. Father Ignacio should be the first to understand that God had shown Miguel a different path.

CHAPTER 17
Homecoming

Captain Riverton was enraged. "What do you mean the footprints lead *toward* the cage?" Two soldiers stood nervously at attention while he shouted at them. "The prisoner's gone, so the prints have to lead *away!*"

Miguel guessed that these must be the guards who had been assigned to watch Rushing Cloud. If they hadn't spent the evening smoking and drinking so far from their prisoner, Miguel would never have been able to help his friend get away.

"That boy was tied hand and foot and locked in," the captain bellowed. "Someone must have set him free, so why isn't there a trail to follow?"

Captain Riverton paced angrily in front of his tent. Cookie busied himself with his breakfast tasks, keeping clear of the captain's wrath. He adjusted the coffeepot as it burbled over the flames. Miguel added a few twigs to the fire and tried to blend in with the camp's bustling activity, but the captain caught sight of him and stepped closer.

"What do you know about all this?" he demanded.

Miguel's head jerked up in surprise. He pretended to be confused. "I just woke up, sir," he said. "I only know what I just heard." Miguel erased all expression from his face. "I might know something about the footprints, though." The captain stared at him, and Miguel tried to look concerned but innocent. "When I was traveling with the Apaches, they never left a campsite without wiping out their prints. Maybe whoever freed the prisoner did the same thing, only he missed some."

The captain scratched the stubble of black and gray whiskers on his unshaven chin. He glared at Miguel with more than a hint of suspicion. Then he turned back to the two sentries.

"This incompetence will not go unpunished," he declared. "I'll deal with you when we return to Fort Lowell." He strode into his tent with a curt, "Dismissed!"

Cookie melted a dollop of bacon grease into a

frying pan. "I bet you know a sight more than you're letting on, eh?"

"Rushing Cloud didn't need any help from me," Miguel lied. "And what could I do with only one good arm?" He cautiously flattened the bulge of rattles in his pocket. "I'll admit I'm glad he's free, though. He didn't do anything wrong."

"All them Indians give me the creeps," Cookie said, breaking two eggs into the pan at once. The fat spattered and spit in all directions. "I just hope we've seen the last of that one."

Miguel was certain they had, and he couldn't help feeling a deep sense of loss mixed with a large dose of satisfaction. He poked around the edges of the camp until it was time for the troop to move out. His shoulder pained him less today, and he realized the medic's treatment must be working. He tried to help Cookie pack the wagon, but at the first movement, the throbbing pain returned. He let Cookie give him a hand getting onto the high wagon seat.

"Giddyap!" the cook called, snapping the reins. With a creak of wheels, the wagon lurched forward. Miguel watched the cavalry formation snaking across the desert. Bright clusters of orange poppies and tufts of feathery purple blooms spread across the sand like a welcoming parade. Tucson lay just over the horizon. As the morning stretched into afternoon, Miguel dozed, lulled by the rocking of the wagon until the distant peal of bells roused him.

Cookie was smiling. "You hear those bells? Somebody's glad you're back."

As the cavalry approached the outskirts of town, the ringing seemed to echo in his chest. At the well, the women set their *ollas* down and ran to welcome the troops. Their *rebozos* streamed behind them in a blur of colors. Miguel had been away so long, but now he was home.

The wagon pulled into town, passing the whitewashed church. Father Ignacio stepped forward, reaching toward Miguel and helping him from the wagon. The clanging bells were deafening, but Miguel was grateful their noise made it difficult to talk. He wouldn't have to explain anything to Father Ignacio, at least not yet. The priest placed his hands on Miguel's head, murmuring a prayer. "Thanks be to God that our Miguel has safely returned to the fold."

Miguel leaned toward the priest's ear and said, "I'm not the same as I was before I was captured. I learned so much while I was in the desert."

Father Ignacio nodded. "You are growing up,

my son, and your world is growing larger. Soon we will talk."

Before Miguel could respond, a crowd surged forward with Miguel's parents in the lead. A lump caught in his throat as his mother engulfed him in her arms, sobbing, and Miguel didn't complain when she squeezed his shoulder in her embrace.

"*Mijo*," she cried. "My son!"

Papá stood close, his eyes moist. "Ah, Miguel," he sighed, reaching out to stroke Miguel's matted hair. "At last you are home. *Gracias a diós.*"

Miguel looked into his father's eyes and felt tears spilling down his cheeks. "Papá," he mumbled. "I didn't understand. I am so sorry."

"We've both had time to think about what we could have done differently," Papá said. "Now we will have time to make things right."

Esteban and Ruben, like two sides of a coin, pushed through the crowd. Esteban was dressed in black finery, and Ruben wore neat work clothes powdered with red desert dust.

"Welcome home, *hermano*. We missed our brother, Miguel!" Ruben hoisted Miguel high onto his shoulder. The crowd cheered and Miguel gazed down into the faces before him—squinting ranchers with their bonneted wives, weathered *campesinos* in white shirts and pants, and Tohono O'odham women balancing burden baskets against their backs. His glance lingered on the faces of the native women. Perhaps one day they might give him news of his friend.

Luis and Berto pushed through the crowd. They whistled and waved to get Miguel's attention. He had worried about whether his friends would turn against him if they learned about his Jewish ancestors. Now he knew that if Berto's ideas didn't change, Miguel couldn't be his friend. Miguel had also been afraid of what Father Ignacio might say. All those worries were in the past.

The sea of people parted as Ruben paraded down the street and set Miguel down in front of the apothecary shop. Charlie Meyer shook Captain Riverton's hand and stepped up onto the wooden walkway. He raised his arms and the crowd fell silent.

"This is a day of celebration for all of us. We thank the Almighty and the US Cavalry for bringing home our son, Miguel Abrano." The people sent up a loud cheer.

One day soon I will tell Doc Meyer about how little the cavalry did, Miguel thought, *and I will tell him about Rushing Cloud.*

He stepped closer to Doc Meyer. With a trembling voice, he said, "Zuzi is gone. Can you forgive me?"

Charlie Meyer's dark eyes narrowed into slits. "You'll work this off, yah?"

Miguel's head drooped. "I'll do whatever it takes to pay you back," he promised. "I can sweep the store as soon as my shoulder heals, and dust the shelves. I'll deliver packages too."

The apothecary bent closer, and Miguel breathed in the familiar scent of pipe tobacco. He lifted Miguel's chin. "It's a tease I am making," he said. "After all, who can worry about an old horse as long as you are safely home? Zuzi's life was nearly over, but yours is just beginning."

Jacob Franck stood just behind Doc Meyer, twisting his round hat in his hands. His hair was neatly cut, and without even looking Miguel knew there had been no horns hiding beneath the peddler's hat. He still wore his long black coat, and his beard sprung out in all directions.

"So brave and strong you are," Señor Franck praised him.

"Not so much as I thought," Miguel said, "but maybe more than I used to be." The peddler hadn't changed at all, but Miguel realized he saw him differently.

Señor Franck cleared his throat and shifted his feet nervously. "I am sorry if I am making so many troubles because of my reading," he apologized. "Maybe I shouldn't be here."

"Oh, no," Miguel said quickly. "I hoped you'd still be in Tucson." He reached out to shake the peddler's hand, feeling its warmth. "Some time before you leave, I—I, that is, would you read the diary to me? I want to hear the whole story this time. I really do. And I'll listen." Maybe he would tell the peddler about Rushing Cloud too.

"Your Papá and I have been working on that book every day," he said. "You can help us write it out in Spanish."

Doc Meyer put his arm around Jacob Franck. "I'm not letting him leave," he announced. "Right here he is staying—in a store right next to mine. Now and then a little cards we'll play and keep up our German. We don't want to forget everything about the Old Country!"

The peddler nodded. "No more housewives waiting months for buttons and blankets. And no more lonely traveling!"

Esteban rode up on his horse, leading the pepper-gray yearling. "We missed your birthday, but we didn't forget," he said. "We knew you had your eye on this one, and Papá says it's time you had your own horse to care for. Hopefully, he'll know the way home if you ever get lost."

Miguel reached up and stroked the horse's neck, and it tossed its long gray mane. They were both descendants of the conquistadors. Miguel would train and care for it until they could race across the desert like the clouds.

Papá gave him a boost into the saddle. The horse pawed the ground, and Miguel leaned forward and whispered, "Easy, Rushing Cloud." The horse perked up its ears. "Yes, that's your name now—Rushing Cloud."

Miguel was certain that his friend's village was welcoming him back too. His family would be proud of how strong and brave Rushing Cloud had been to leave the mission school and cross the desert alone. *Well, almost alone*, he thought.

He looked out across the crush of people. How good it was to hear the voices of his family and friends. Before him, the many faces of Tucson melted into one.

AFTERWORD

Arizona Territory was still a desert settlement in 1872 when the story *Walk Till You Disappear* takes place. The city of Tucson had just three thousand residents, most of them of Mexican heritage. Many could trace their family lineage back to the sixteenth century when the Spanish adventurer Hernando Cortés arrived in the newly discovered land with his army of conquistadors. Cortés and his soldiers claimed the land in the name of Spain and the Catholic Church, killing many of the native people and forcing many more to convert.

The brush huts of the Tohono O'odham, mistakenly called the Papago tribe, dotted the land. These Native Americans lived peacefully in their scattered villages, farming small fields and selling their beautifully crafted baskets and pottery in the settlement towns. Their water jugs, called *ollas* by the Mexicans, were famous for their ability to keep water cool throughout a hot desert day. As more settlers moved in to the territory, mission schools opened, run by different church groups. They worked with the US government to take Native American children from their families, and "Americanize" them. While Arizona didn't have many mission schools before 1891, I took some liberties in describing the experiences of many Native American boys and girls through Rushing Cloud's story.

In the ninteenth century, Tucson was the only fortified walled town in America. It had to fight off attacks by Mexican bandits, Apache raiders, and gunslinging outlaws. Tucson had a dusty main street, a brewery and some saloons, one café, and several low adobe buildings. One of its most highly respected residents was Charles Meyer, a German immigrant who ran the town's only apothecary shop and was fondly called Doc Meyer for his vast knowledge of medicines. In 1864 he also became justice of the peace, serving as judge and jailer of the city's lawbreakers.

By 1872, when young Miguel might have lived there, Tucson had been part of the United States less than twenty years. The annexation happened in 1854, when President Franklin Pierce signed an agreement called the Gadsden Purchase. Under this contract, Mexico sold land to the United States in what is now the southern portion of Arizona and New Mexico. Overnight, all the Mexicans and the native people living in the area became American citizens—whether they wished to or not.

Arizona Territory wanted desperately to become a full-fledged state, but the Congress in Washington, DC, repeatedly refused. The territory's leaders were certain that if they established public schools, it would help their push for statehood. So, in 1871, Tucson built the town's first public school for boys. The residents also wanted the newest citizens, who had so recently been Mexican, to learn English and study the government of the United States. Schools were the best way to accomplish those goals.

Settlers continued to arrive in the territory, some of them immigrants from European countries. Most of the time, they were met with acceptance and tolerance. But sometimes they faced hostile residents who didn't like foreigners or those of a different faith. Tucson's only house of worship was a small Catholic mission that offered weekly Mass and tried to convert newcomers and the native people. There were few Jewish settlers in the Southwest, but those that did arrive mostly overcame lingering prejudices to become successful in business and politics.

Arizona Territory was growing steadily toward statehood. Its population continued to rise as ranchers, merchants, and cattlemen braved its many dangers to make a new life for themselves and their families.

GLOSSARY

adiós: (ah-dee-OHS) Spanish—goodbye

adobe: (uh-DOH-bee) Spanish—a brick made of straw and clay

agave: (AH-guh-vay) Spanish—a desert plant with spiky leaves

apothecary: (uh-POTH-uh-carry) English—a pharmacist

bar mitzvah: (bahr MITZ-vuh) Hebrew—a Jewish boy who reaches the age of thirteen and is considered an adult

bien: (byen) Spanish—good

bimuelo: (beem-WELL-oh) Spanish—a flaky pastry that is fried in oil and then sprinkled with sugar and cinnamon

brittle bush: English—a shrub that grows in dry areas. Its leaves are gray green, and it has yellow flowers.

campesino: Spanish—a farmer; someone who lives in the countryside and works the land *charco*: (CHAR-ko) Spanish—a depression in the land that holds water; a pond

conquistadors: (kon-KEES-ta-DORS) Spanish—conquerors; victorious soldiers

converso: (kon-VER-so) Spanish—a person who has converted to another religion; one who pretends to convert

creosote: (CREE-uh-sote) English—a fragrant bush with bright yellow flowers common in the desert Southwest

Doña: (DOHN-ya) Spanish—a title of respect used with the first name of a woman

exactamente: (eh-zact-uh-MEN-tay) Spanish—exactly

excelente: (eh-zeh-LEN-tay) Spanish—excellent

fiesta: (fee-ES-tuh) Spanish—party; celebration

gracias a diós: (GRAH-see-ahs ah DEE-ohs) Spanish—thank God

hasta: (HAH-stah) Spanish—until

hermano: (air-MAH-noh) Spanish—brother

hobble: English—a rope or other device used to keep an animal from walking

hola: (OH-lah) Spanish—hi; hello

I'itoi: (ee-ee-toy)—Tohono O'odham name meaning "Elder Brother," who is believed to be one of the four creators of the world

Inquisition: English—a panel of Roman Catholic judges who investigated those accused of not following the church's teachings

javelina: (hah-veh-LEAN-uh)—wild boar

mañana: (mahn-YA-nah) Spanish—tomorrow

mantilla: (mahn-TEE-ya) Spanish—a lacy head covering

mesquite: (meh-SKEET) Spanish—a small spiny tree native to the Southwest. It grows edible pods that are part of the pea family.

mijo: (MEE-ho) Spanish—conjoined term of *mi hijo,* meaning "my son"

milagro: (mih-LAH-grow) Spanish—miracle

no me digas: (no meh DEE-gaz) Spanish—you don't say

olla: (OY-ya) Spanish—a clay jug to hold water

padre: (PAH-dray) Spanish—father

paloverde: (PAH-lo VAIR-deh) Spanish—literally "green bark"; a desert tree with lime-green bark

patina: (PAT-ee-nuh)—a plate used during the Catholic Communion service

Pima: (PEE-muh)—a Southwest desert tribe

pinole: (pee-NOH-lay) Spanish—a ground meal made with mesquite beans, corn, and wheat

prickly pear: English—a variety of cactus with oval, flat, spiny pads

¿qué pasa?: (kay PAH-sah) Spanish—What happened?

¿quién pasa?: (kyen PAH-sah) Spanish—Who's there?

quiver: English—a carrying bag for arrows

ramada: (ruh-MAH-duh) Spanish—an open area covered by a trellis to provide shade

rancheria: (rahn-cheh-REE-uh) Spanish—a small village with several small huts

rebozo: (reh-BO-zo) Spanish—a shawl

saguaro: (suh-WAH-row) Spanish—a large cactus with waxy, white flowers that produces an edible red fruit

señor/señorita: (sehn-YOR/sehn-yoh-REE-tah) Spanish—Mister/Miss

Tohono O'odham: (teh-hono-OH-tahm)—a Southwest desert tribe

Torah: (TOH-rah) Hebrew—a scroll containing the first five books of the Hebrew Scriptures

vámanos: (VAH-mah-nohs) Spanish—Let's go

Yo soy: (yoh soy) Spanish—I am

zopilote: (zoh-pill-LO-teh) Spanish—a small American black vulture

BIBLIOGRAPHY

Fontana, Bernard. "The Papágos." *Arizona Highways*, April 1983, 34.

Greene, Jacqueline Dembar. *The Tohono O'odham*. New York: Franklin Watts, 1998.

Hoim, Tom (Cherokee/Creek). "Warriors and Warfare." In *Encyclopedia of North American Indians*, edited by Frederick Hokie, 666. New York: Houghton Mifflin, 1996.

Libo, Kenneth, and Irving Howe. *We Lived There, Too*. New York: St. Martin's Press, 1984.

Lockwood, Frank C. *Pioneer Portraits*. Tucson: University of Arizona Press, 1968.

McCarthy, James. *A Papágo Traveler*. Tucson: University of Arizona Press, 1985.

Melody, Michael E. *The Apache*. New York: Chelsea House 1988.

Monaghan, Jay, ed. *The Book of the American West*. New York: Julian Messner, 1963.

Miner, Carrie M. "Road Runner: Facts and Fantasy." *Arizona Highways*, April 2001, 14.

Muel, Chips. "Left for Dead," *Arizona Highways*, February, 1992, 12.

Nabhan, Gary Paul. *The Desert Smells Like Rain*. San Francisco: North Point, 1982.

Rischin, Moses, and John Livingston. *Jews of the American West*. Detroit: Wayne State University Press, 1991.

Roberts, Virginia Culin. *With Their Own Blood*. Fort Worth, TX: Christian University Press, 1972.

Trimble, Marshall. *Arizona*. New York: Doubleday, 1977.

Trover, Ellen Lloyd, and William F. Swindler. *Chronology and Documentary Handbook of the State of Arizona*. Dobbs Ferry, NY: Oceana, 1972.

Tyler, Hamilton A. *Pueblo Birds and Myths*. Flagstaff, AZ: Northland, 1991.

Underhill, Ruth. *Singing for Power*. Tucson: University of Arizona Press, 1993.

White, Anne Terry. *The American Indian*. New York: Random House, 1963.

ABOUT THE AUTHOR

Jacqueline Dembar Greene is the award-winning author of more than forty books for young readers, including American Girl's® Rebecca Rubin series and *The Secret Shofar of Barcelona*. She lives in Wayland, Massachusetts.